TW... ...live!

ng.

Lil ... her
be ... rab
ma ... ssi-
ble ... en
ma ... ow
cou

... ing
a p ... ere
ha ... be!

... the
ins ... ve-
me ... he
sca ... oin
up ... en
it ... if
gat

... on
the ... the
liv ... he
sca ... nie
bru ... he
flo ... in,
wh

... d,
lea ... in
sho

**Books by John Peel**

TALONS
SHATTERED

**Available from ARCHWAY Paperbacks**

# SHATTERED

## JOHN PEEL

**AN ARCHWAY PAPERBACK**
Published by POCKET BOOKS

New York   London   Toronto   Sydney   Tokyo   Singapore

This book is a work of fiction. Names, characters, places and
incidents are either products of the author's imagination or are used
fictitiously. Any resemblance to actual events or locales or persons,
living or dead, is entirely coincidental.

An ARCHWAY PAPERBACK *Original*

An Archway Paperback published by
POCKET BOOKS, a division of Simon & Schuster Inc.
1230 Avenue of the Americas, New York, NY 10020

ISBN: 0-671-79406-X

First Archway Paperback printing December 1993

10  9  8  7  6  5  4  3  2  1

AN ARCHWAY PAPERBACK and colophon are
registered trademarks of Simon & Schuster Inc.

Cover art by Lisa Falkenstern

Printed in the U.S.A.

IL 7+

*For Shana David*

# SHATTERED

# PROLOGUE

*I thirst.*

The old man felt rather than heard the voice at the corner of his mind. His lip curled slightly. "Patience," he whispered. "One will come."

*How long must I wait?* asked the voice. *It has been too long already.*

The old man rose from his work at the counter. He strode past the shadowy objects that lurked about his store until he stood by the glass door. "We have to wait," he said softly. "In the last town we were almost caught. You were too greedy." He stared out of the door and into the mall beyond. The store was dark and oppressive; the mall wide and bright. It was new, lively, and filled with life. People hurried back and forth, clutching packages, sipping drinks, laughing, and chattering.

No sound disturbed the stillness of the store, though. The air inside, dead and heavy, was silent. The old man's eyes sparkled as he watched the teenagers outside joking and talking. Their bodies were so fresh and young, so filled with the energy of life.

It was wasted on them. They couldn't appreciate their vitality—but *he* could. And so could the owner of the voice.

*Life,* whispered the voice, seeing what he could see. *I can almost taste it now.*

"Patience," the man repeated. "I have begun. The call has gone out. One will come shortly—one who will be perfect for our needs, who will help quench your thirst."

*How soon?* The voice was almost begging now. *How much longer must I wait before I drink of life again?*

"Not long," the old man promised. He considered the matter. "Tonight," he finally said, and gestured out at the young people passing by. The shoppers and mall rats, who didn't even spare his store a second glance, were unaware of anyone watching them. "The one who will come is out there. I can feel her approaching even now. She will come, I promise."

*And then I shall drink,* the voice whispered eagerly.

"Yes," he promised. "Then you shall drink—the first of many in this town." With satisfaction and anticipation gleaming in his ancient eyes, he turned away from the window. "Very soon," he murmured. "And then we both shall have what we need."

# CHAPTER
# 1

~<

"This place terrifies me."

Stephanie Kirk glanced over at her friend Nicola
—"everybody-calls-me-Nicky-or-else!"—Powers and
rolled her eyes. "I need a break," Stephanie begged.

"You're on one," Nicki pointed out, collapsing into
a wooden folding chair beside Stephanie. After pulling off her Burger Heaven hat, she shook out her
shaggy, medium-length black hair. "For about another minute and a half," she added.

Checking her watch, Stephanie realized that Nicki
was correct. Her break was almost over, and it was
just about time to head back out of the cramped
employees' lounge and into the fray of the fast-food

world. When the new Greenfields Mall had opened two months earlier, the chance of getting an after-school job at the Burger Heaven outlet had seemed like a terrific opportunity. A great way to earn a little extra cash and a chance to hang out in the coolest new mall in the entire state. After seven weeks on the job, though, Stephanie was definitely regretting the decision.

Part of the reason was that the restaurant—too grand a word for the place—attracted the most obnoxious customers in the world. A larger part of the reason was the overbearing supervisor, Henry Blake. Nicki swore he worked there only because there weren't any openings in the Spanish Inquisition. Nicki was famous for overstating everything, but in this case she wasn't far off the mark. Blake just seemed to love to torture his employees. Stephanie tried to ignore his abuse and get along with him, but that was difficult. He provoked confrontations and enjoyed sneering at the other workers.

With a sigh, Stephanie examined her reflection in the small mirror on the wall beside the bulletin board, which was littered with the required health warnings, employee notices, and Blake's irritating memos. She looked a little tired as she twisted her long, blond braid into a bun, pinned it into place, and then put on her Burger Heaven hat.

"This is a great training place for life," she commented. "It teaches you not to expect too much."

"Don't interrupt me," Nicki complained, glancing

up from the pages of her latest romance novel. "I'm on my break."

Stephanie shook her head and pushed open the door. Instantly the stench of hot oil, seared meat, and overcooked chicken hit her in the face. Her fellow employees were rushing about, trying to keep up with the constant stream of orders. One of the other girls from her class who worked there, Paka Tracy, gave her a quick grin.

"Am I glad to see you," Paka said, bobbing her head toward the counter. Her long dreadlocks were tied off with small bells that tinkled as she moved. "This place is crazy." To the harassed cooks, she yelled, "Where's my order of chicken pieces?"

"On my way," Stephanie promised, heading back to the register she was working. With a wince she ground to a halt as her path was blocked by Henry Blake.

Blake was only a few years older than the girls, and he took his "rank" far too seriously. He'd studied restaurant management after leaving school. Despite his youth, he had already started to lose his thin, wispy blond hair. As a result, he combed it across the crown of his head, accentuating the problem instead of hiding it. Perhaps it was sensitivity over his hair loss that made him so testy, Stephanie argued. Nicki maintained that it was just inborn nastiness.

"Kirk," he snapped. "Nice to see you back."

"And on time," she added in as sweet a voice as she could manage. "If you let me get out to the counter, I'll help with this crowd." Over his shoulder she could see four long lines at the counter. The dining area beyond looked crowded, too.

"Not yet," he told her. "There's been a spill on the floor beside table seventeen. I want you to clean it up before someone slips and sues us."

Swallowing hard, Stephanie held down her annoyance. For some reason Blake enjoyed making her do such menial chores. "Okay," she said with no enthusiasm. "I'll get on it right away."

"See that you do." Blake gave her a quick nod, then moved off.

"Stephanie," Paka said, "you are just too easygoing, you know that? He's taking advantage of you."

"There's no point in getting worked up about it," Stephanie replied, picking up a cleaning scoop, a plastic bag, a mop, and a bucket of water. "It'll only make him act worse."

"Maybe." Paka's grin was pure white against her dark skin. "If he ordered *me* around like that, I'd find a better place to stick that mop handle."

Stephanie managed a weak grin at this, then trudged out from the kitchen area into the dining room.

The place was packed. Beyond the large windows she could see that the mall was doing its usual brisk Sunday business, and a number of families and solo shoppers were drifting in for a fast bite before continuing their search for the ultimate bargain. Most of the tables had diners at them—noisy, sloppy, and often disgusting eaters. Stephanie steeled herself not to look as she headed for table seventeen. Some little kids were hurling french fries about, but she managed to dodge the ones thrown in her direction.

"Mess" was an understatement, she realized, as she approached the table. It looked as if a small war had been fought there. A ketchup bottle had been smashed on the floor, and bits of food and glass stuck up like shrapnel from the gooey mess. The culprits had long since vanished, of course. Her heart sinking, Stephanie got down on her hands and knees and used the cleaning scoop to scrape up most of the ketchup, food, and broken glass. Then she dumped it in the plastic garbage bag and cleaned up the spill area with the mop. As she scrubbed away, she heard an all-too-familiar voice behind her.

"Well, Stephanie, I see you've risen to your natural level—on your hands and knees."

Stephanie glanced back over her shoulder. As she'd dreaded, there stood Kimberly Cullum with her kept-on-a-tight-leash boyfriend, David Blaise. Kimberly's father was one of the wealthiest men in the state, if not the country, and she used her family wealth and standing to beat other kids over the head. "Hello, Kimberly," she said. "I didn't know you ate here."

*"Moi?"* Kimberly laughed. "What an idea." She looked around in disgust. "We just saw you groveling in the grime and thought we'd tell you how well it suits you."

"You're all heart." Stephanie concentrated on the task at hand, trying to stop her flush of embarrassment from growing more intense. No doubt Kimberly would spread the story at school in the morning, and everyone who wanted to stay in good with her would be certain to mention it to Stephanie and laugh.

"One of my few failings," agreed Kimberly. She tossed her long jet-black hair and wrinkled her petite nose fastidiously. "God, the stench in this place is making me nauseous."

"Don't let me keep you," muttered Stephanie.

"I won't." Using her exquisitely manicured nails, Kimberly flicked a stray lock of hair from her eyes. "If you need more work, I believe my father has an opening for a new cleaner. You look so natural like that." She spun on her heel. "Come along, David. If I stay here any longer, I'll be sick."

*You make me sick,* Stephanie thought. What an obnoxious snob the girl was. It took all of her will-power not to answer her back as meanly. But there wasn't any point in that; it would only intensify Kimberly's antagonism. Best just to act as if she weren't affected by the other girl. Stephanie scrubbed away at the floor, wishing it were Kimberly's face. . . .

Something hit her on her calf and bounced onto the floor next to her. She looked up and saw an apologetic-looking young mother holding on to a two-year-old at the next table. The small boy was screaming and had started to throw his food around. A messy portion of his hamburger had smacked into Stephanie's leg, smearing ketchup and grease across her nylons. *Ru-ined,* she thought, miserably, and now she had another mess to clean up. What a terrific day this was turning out to be.

Kimberly strode through the mall feeling rather pleased with herself. She'd never liked Stephanie Kirk. Stephanie always managed to get better grades in all their classes, and she never realized that Kimberly was *better* than she. Those sweet little responses of hers didn't fool Kimberly for one second; Stephanie envied her, that was more than obvious.

Well, she had good reason to be envious. Kimberly paused to examine her reflection in the window of a card store. She liked what she saw—five feet seven inches of class and undiluted sex appeal. Her hair was perfect, flowing down to her shoulders in soft waves and curls. Her skin was perfect—just tan enough to make it apparent that she took her vacations in the Bahamas, Hawaii, or the Mediterranean, not Disney World or Newport News. Her clothes were perfect, too, of course, and accentuated her trim to-die-for figure. Yes, there was plenty about her for Stephanie to envy. And why not? Didn't *everyone* envy her?

Then she caught sight of David's reflection. He was hovering nervously next to her as he always did. David was just a couple of inches taller than she, with neatly cropped light brown—almost sandy—hair. His skin was paler than Kimberly's but just as free of blemishes. The idea of being seen with someone who had zits was too repugnant to contemplate! His family wasn't as affluent as hers, but whose was? Still, the

Blaises did all right. His father managed the largest brokerage firm in town, and his mother dominated the social scene—after Mrs. Cullum, naturally.

"Don't drool, David," Kimberly said with a sigh. Being beautiful did have its drawbacks. Boys made such a nuisance of themselves at times. Still, one of the reasons she kept David around was that he was attentive.

"Um, I was just . . ." he said nervously, not finishing his sentence.

"I could see what you were *just,*" she replied. "I'll let you know when I want to be adored, okay?" Without waiting for a reply, she took off. David, as was proper, fell in beside her. That was another reason she liked having him around—not only did he look good but he knew his place as well.

The mall was crowded, and Kimberly disliked crowds. Normally, of course, she would not shop in such a vulgar place. The mall was for common people, not Cullums! But her father owned a substantial slice of this place, and she occasionally enjoyed seeing his money grow. And the stress of dealing with the crowds was more than made up for by that delightful encounter with Stephanie Kirk. She marched on, barely glancing at the stores as she passed them. Whatever they sold could hardly be of interest to her. And she avoided looking at the people, who actually seemed to—she shuddered—*enjoy* this place. That was the trouble with the world—so many common people with low-brow tastes and pleasures.

Then she stopped dead in her tracks. David almost

walked into her as she gave another shiver of disgust. "What is *that* place?" she asked, staring at the small store in front of her.

David stared at the shop uncertainly. "It looks like an antique store," he offered helpfully.

"It looks like a *landfill,*" Kimberly said and sneered. "How on earth could the mall management have let something so—tacky in here?"

Considering the fact that the mall was only two months old, it was almost beyond belief that a store so disgusting had managed to spring into being. The paint on the facade was chipped in several places already. The color scheme was dirty brown and faded orange, and the place bore only a simple sign: Dolman Antiques. In the large plate-glass window numerous artifacts were displayed in front of a black backdrop. Arranged on a bookcase and two tables was an assortment of what could only be described as junk— a vase with a cracked glaze; a horrendous Chinese porcelain pug dog with some of the paint missing; a large, dark Japanese screen that had probably been in someone's basement for a decade, judging from the amount of mildew on it; several Tiffany-style lamps, their stained-glass panels dulled with age and lack of care. There was a variety of other items she couldn't begin to classify, and a whole row of ancient medicine bottles in dirty green, brown, and blue. There were china plates and dishes that didn't quite make up sets. There were even a couple of battered and faded dolls that looked as if they'd been buried for a couple of hundred years, and then carelessly hosed down.

It was clearly not the kind of store that belonged in the mall! She would have to speak to her father about getting the lease terminated. The thing to do was to collect one of the business cards for the dump and then alert her father to its existence. Steeling herself, Kimberly stormed into the store with David at her heels.

The gloom was almost palpable. It seemed to ooze out of the scattered objects in the sales room and settle around her like thick fog. All of the other stores were brightly lit, but the owner of this one had allowed the lightbulbs to burn out or perhaps had even painted them over. Accompanying the dismal lighting was . . . well, *stench* was too mild a word for it. It was the sort of damp stink that old books and houses sometimes acquired. The smell of decay, age, and disease. Kimberly wrinkled her nose, wondering what sort of damage she was doing to her lungs just by breathing.

Inside was just as depressing as out. There were a couple of battered suits of armor on guard duty near the entrance. Shelves along the walls were littered with items that were supposed to be antiques but looked more like the things found in garbage dumps. The larger pieces included some old trunks and tables and even a cradle that hadn't been new two hundred years earlier. A stack of old issues of *Life* magazine spilled over from an occasional table. Large floor lamps with faded silk shades stood unplugged and unloved. She noticed a box of old presidential campaign buttons on one table and a pile of old toys from

TV shows on another. Kimberly almost gagged on the putrid smell that rose around her.

On a small table set off to one side was an ancient cash register. It was a turn-of-the-century model with large keys to strike to make tiny numbers snap up into the glass screen at the top of the bulky relic. Beside it was a small box containing business cards. Stephanie picked one up using just the tips of her nails and slipped it into her wallet. She was just closing the wallet with a decisive snap when she heard a shuffling sound from the back room, and the owner of the store appeared.

He looked even worse—if it was possible—than the store itself. His thin body, twisted as if his spine were curved, barely filled out his faded and patched clothes. His skin was blotched by liver spots, and there was not enough hair on his head for Kimberly to guess what color it might have once been. Old square-lens spectacles were perched at the end of his beaklike nose. The moles on his face included one that sprouted several long hairs. His jaw was covered with uneven stubble, as if he'd shaved in the dark and missed his face as often as he hit it. When he spoke, she could see gaps between his teeth. "Can I help you?"

"I sincerely doubt it," she replied, pulling back in disgust. This made her collide with David, who stumbled.

"Careful!" the old man exclaimed. "You'll break things!"

"Who'd miss them?" Kimberly asked. "You've got some nerve trying to sell junk like this to the public."

The old man stared at her with weak, watery blue eyes. "I supply what some people enjoy," he said. "Treasures of the past."

"Treasures?" she scoffed. "This place should be burned down as a health hazard. I doubt that even one thing in this entire store is worth a second glance."

The shopkeeper didn't seem offended by her words. "You know something about antiques, then?" he asked.

"Something," she agreed. "And this is all just junk."

"I know a little myself," he said, moving to one of the shelves.

"You look as if you belong beside the suits of armor," Kimberly snapped.

He considered the comment. "I might at that," he agreed, still not at all upset. "They're all a part of me, and I'm a part of them." He reached up to the shelf and took something down. "Would you care to give me an expert opinion on this little item, young lady?" He held it out for her to take.

Kimberly's first reaction was to pull away for fear that the millions of germs on the thing might suddenly leap out and infect her. But then her curiosity got the better of her, and she leaned forward, puzzled. The old man held a mirror out to her, and she frowned as she took it and examined it.

It was about ten inches long. The handle was of

some old metal—possibly silver, more likely plated brass—and was shaped like a twisted candle, spiraling up and separating around the mirror, which was pure and clean, giving back a perfect reflection. On the frame was some kind of elfin or fairy creature, wings and hands spread out around the looking glass. The sprite, with its slanted brows and eyes and its cheery, almost wicked grin, was neither male nor female. Its eyes were two small blue gemstones.

Kimberly knew immediately that this was a genuine work of art. Her father prided himself on his gifts to museums and had exposed her to enough treasures to give her a good understanding of the value of things. This was a one-of-a-kind piece, handcrafted with skill and care. Its age only made it more valuable. Finding it in a place like this was about as likely as finding a diamond in the stomach of a frog.

"Nice, isn't it?" asked the old man.

"Maybe," she agreed guardedly. It was possible that the idiot didn't know what he had. He'd probably found it in a bunch of useless junk he'd bought and simply liked the look of it.

"Would you care to buy it?" he suggested, watching her carefully.

"No." She started to hand it back, then reconsidered. It might just be quite valuable, and she'd hate to lose the chance of owning it. On the other hand, she didn't want to seem too eager, or he'd raise the price. She caught sight of her own reflection and noticed that the mirror seemed to enhance her striking looks. A very flattering glass, even given the perfection of her face. "How much?"

"Twelve hundred dollars."

She stared at him, aghast. "You must be joking," she snapped. It was possible—even likely—that the mirror was worth more than that. But she had absolutely no intention of paying such a price.

"It's a real work of art," the old man said with a whine in his voice.

Kimberly's eyes narrowed shrewdly. This place was empty except for the three of them. He probably didn't get many customers—even the common hordes couldn't find this sort of thing attractive, no matter how unrefined their taste—so he was probably strapped for money, in which case, he'd take considerably less than the mirror was worth. "I wouldn't give you a hundred for it," she replied.

"A hundred?" The storekeeper acted appalled. "Surely you must realize that it's worth twenty times that!"

David peered over her shoulder. "It might be valuable," he offered apologetically.

"Who asked you?" Kimberly snapped. Didn't David know any better than that? *Never* admit that something you're offered might be worth money—the first rule of bargaining. And *never* sound interested. Honestly, he should have known better by now. She'd have to remind him later to keep his mouth firmly closed in the future. Handing the mirror back to the proprietor, she said coldly: "It's nothing to me." She started to turn, certain he wouldn't let her get away. She was correct.

He started to reach out for her arm, but a withering look from her stopped his hand. "Eight hundred," he suggested.

Kimberly sniffed loudly. "I don't intend to bargain with you," she said. "I'll give you two hundred and no more. Take it or leave it." She could see the indecision written over his repulsive face. She knew he was right—the mirror was worth far more than she'd offered—but she also knew he was in dire need of cash. "Come along, David," she said. "We'd better be going."

"All right," the old man said quickly. "Two hundred it is. But you're robbing me, and you know it."

"I'm giving you charity," she replied, tossing her head, "and *you* know it." She reached into her purse for her wallet. Luckily, she had a lot of cash with her. She never knew when it might be useful.

The old man—Dolman, she guessed his name was—scurried into the back room. "I'll put it in a box for you," he called back. "Just a moment."

Kimberly sighed. It was pathetic, really—the old bait-and-switch routine. He would come back with a box all ready to go—containing something other than the mirror she was buying. He was relying on her stupidity and greed to make her want to leave immediately, and she was not supposed to discover the switch until she got home. Then she'd be too ashamed to tell anyone. Honestly! She carefully counted out two hundred dollars and held the money in her hand. She barely noticed that David was still hovering behind her.

Dolman came out of the back room with a gift box clutched in his dirty hands. "Here we are," he said briskly. He held it out in one hand, reaching for the money with the other. Kimberly waited till he almost had it, then jerked it back, out of his reach.

"Open it up," she ordered.

"What?" The old man appeared cornered, almost scared.

"You heard me," she told him. "I want another look at my mirror."

"But—but I just boxed it," he protested.

"I'm sure you did," she agreed, feeling rather pleased with herself. "But I'd like to make certain you didn't damage it before I leave."

Guilt and worry were reflected in his eyes as he pulled the top off the box. Inside it was a nest of tissue paper. "You're sure?" he asked nervously.

"Quite sure."

Biting his lip, Dolman carefully pulled back the layers of tissue paper to expose what lay within.

The mirror.

Kimberly frowned, genuinely surprised. "But—" She saw the malicious smile that flickered across Dolman's face. He'd *meant* her to make a fool of her! He'd been playing with her! Flushing furiously, she slapped the cash down on the table. "There's the money."

He handed her the open box. "And here's the mirror you've bought," he said mildly.

Snatching it from his hands, Kimberly pushed the tissue paper back into the box and jammed the lid on it again. Without saying another word, she spun around and stormed out of the store, David following close on her heels.

Dolman watched them leave, the amused smile still on his face. He picked up the money and slipped the bills into his vest pocket. As soon as the icy, mean girl was out of sight, he shuffled back into the rear room of the store.

On the table there lay the real mirror that the girl thought she'd purchased. It was a beautiful work of art, one of the best items he'd ever made. It had taken him a week, but it had been time well spent. Behind the table was a full-length mirror in a stand. A cloth was draped over the looking glass, revealing only the shape of the piece. *That* was the real treasure in this store—not that anyone would ever guess.

He picked up the hand mirror. He'd have to keep it in the back for a couple of days, until that girl was dealt with. Then he could put it out on sale again. He smiled once more. That foolish child had thought she could get the better of the bargain! What arrogance in one so young and stupid! Well, she'd learn. She'd have a little time for—he chuckled at the joke—reflection!

Then . . . well, then she'd die, of course. Which was what he needed. He glanced at his reflection in the hand mirror. He'd seen better days—and he'd see better days again soon.

Very, very soon. He knew that was certain.

# CHAPTER 2

She was going to die.

Stephanie pulled the ruined panty hose off her aching legs, wadded them up, and threw them into the trash container in the tiny women's room. She felt so utterly weary that she didn't know if she had the strength to limp out to Nicki's car. And she knew that the next day she'd be the laughingstock of the school, thanks to Kimberly Cullum. What a day to look forward to. The day she'd die of embarrassment.

With a heavy heart and heavier feet, Stephanie managed to get herself into gear, propelling herself out of the women's room and through the still-busy dining room of Burger Heaven. If all good things came to an end, fortunately so did all bad ones—like her shift.

The mall would be open for another three hours, but she and Nicki were finished for the day. Paka waved to her from behind the counter, and she managed a quick wave back. Trying to ignore the crowd, Stephanie made her way to the parking lot. It took her a minute to picture where Nicki had parked in the crowded lot, but then she remembered and crossed to the deep blue Ford Taurus that was her friend's pride and joy. Stephanie wished she could afford a car—any car!—but since her mom had lost her job, money had been tight in her family. Maybe when the job situation in town picked up and there was a need for graphic artists again they'd be able to afford one. Till then, at least, Nicki was there for her.

As Stephanie collapsed into the passenger seat, Nicki shook her head. "You look terrible," she commented.

"Thanks," said Stephanie, sighing and laying her head back wearily. "You have no idea how much it cheers me to hear that."

"Anytime." Nicki started the car and backed out of the parking spot. "What else are friends for?" She steered her way through pedestrians who were convinced they didn't need to watch out for traffic. "Look, Steph, why don't you tell Blake to shove it? He's really picking on you, and you know it."

"I need the job," Stephanie replied, not willing to admit how tempting the idea sounded. "My money really does help out at home."

"Yeah, but look at what it's doing to you," her

friend pointed out. "What's the good of ruining your clothes and your health over a lousy job in a burger joint? Not to mention your pride and your nerves?"

"I can't afford pride and nerves," Stephanie answered.

Nicki acted concerned. "If you weren't my best friend," she said, "I'd tell you that you're a wimp. You let people walk all over you." She grinned. "Even me."

"If you weren't my best friend," Stephanie replied, "I'd say you could be right. I don't have the energy to argue."

Nicki sighed. "Get some rest, then, but don't snore too loud. It distracts me from driving."

Neither of them lived far from the mall, so the drive took only fifteen minutes. Most of it was accompanied by Nicki's cheery ramblings about anything that struck her. She was completely unaffected by the lack of response from Stephanie. Nothing seemed to get Nicki down, and her reserves of energy were astonishing. She was almost as fresh as she had been when the day began. If Stephanie had had any strength left, she might have resented her friend's resilience. As it was, she simply let Nicki's waves of chatter wash over her.

Nicki pulled up in front of the Kirk house—a small ranch on a quiet street. Nicki lived just a couple of blocks away in a very similar house. With a grin, she asked, "Want me to carry you up to the door, or do you think you can make it alone?"

Stephanie grimaced. "I'll do my best. If I'm not at school tomorrow, you'll know I collapsed on the way in."

"Just think," Nicki called as Stephanie clambered out of the car. "These are the best years of your life."

"I know. That's what terrifies me." She managed a halfhearted wave as Nicki drove off. She opened the gate in the chain-link fence and walked up to the front door. The house was small, but large enough for her family. There were only Stephanie and her younger sister, Shelly, and the family dog, Montmorency, or Monty, to share the place with her parents. After stumbling inside, she saw her mother working over some papers on the coffee table in the living room. Monty was on the carpet beside her, sleeping as usual. He was a rather scruffy terrier of indeterminate breed, mostly white with patches of brown and black. He managed to open one eye and raise his head an inch or two to check her out before falling back asleep.

"You and me both," she told him.

"Hi, sweetheart," her mother said, glancing up from her papers. "Rough day?"

"You could say that," Stephanie replied, giving her a quick kiss on the cheek. "About like most of my days." She kicked off her shoes and sighed with relief. "Anything new?"

Her mother brushed her own corn gold hair out of her eyes. They looked very much alike, really, and Stephanie had clearly inherited her mother's good looks and, possibly, her brains. "Well, Scott called."

Her boyfriend. Stephanie winced. "He doesn't want

to see me tonight, does he?" she asked. Normally she enjoyed his company, but that night she just wanted to curl up somewhere comfortable and die.

"No." Mrs. Kirk gave her daughter a shrewd look. "He asked me to ask you to please remember to bring his history notes with you tomorrow."

"Oh, yeah." Stephanie had forgotten she'd borrowed them. "He loaned them to me to catch up," she explained. She'd had a cold a couple of weeks back and missed two days while she recovered. "I'll pack them, promise."

"Good." Then her mother smiled. "And I had some good news today. The personnel manager of Martinson's gave me a call. They're looking for a new art director, and I'm hired on three months' probation. They even saw me today, on Sunday."

"That's terrific, Mom!" Stephanie hugged her mother. It would be wonderful. She knew that the probation would be just a formality. Her mother was great at her work. Since she'd been laid off, she'd been very depressed. This should recharge her spiritual batteries! "When do you start?"

"Tomorrow." Mrs. Kirk gestured at the table. "That's why I'm going over all this stuff. I picked it up today. They really must be keen on me if they saw me on Sunday, so I want to charge in tomorrow morning full of great ideas."

"You always have great ideas," Stephanie replied. She glanced around. "What did you do with Dad?"

"I needed some peace, so I sent him bowling." Mrs. Kirk grinned. "It didn't take much persuasion! And your sister is in her room, with strict orders not to bother me. And now that you're home, the same goes for you."

"Believe me," Stephanie said, "I haven't got the energy to annoy anyone." She walked slowly to her small and rather cramped bedroom, threw her coat across her chair, and collapsed onto her bed. It felt really good not to be vertical any longer. She'd just rest for a minute, then change out of her uniform. . . .

The door to her sister's room across the hallway opened, and Shelly popped out. She was thirteen, and as unlike Stephanie as anyone could be. Her hair was a mass of dark brown curls, her face a little round. She looked vaguely like a cherub, but looks were as far as it went. "Old age catching up with you?" she asked unsympathetically.

Stephanie opened one eye and fixed it on her sister. "Isn't that my sweater?" she asked.

Shelly barely glanced down at the light pink knit she was wearing. "You weren't wearing it," she replied, "and it looks better on me, anyway. I've got more of a figure than you."

"You should still ask before you borrow things," Stephanie scolded. "How many more of my things have you taken?"

"If you can't keep track of your clothes, I'm not going to tell you," Shelly answered haughtily.

"I'd appreciate your returning my stuff," Stephanie commented, sitting up on the bed. "And not taking any more."

"Suit yourself." Shelly pulled the sweater over her

head and dumped it on the floor. Under it, she wore one of her Michael Jackson T-shirts. As Stephanie fished up the discarded sweater, Shelly retreated to her room and closed the door.

Stephanie shook her head. Had *she* been that impossible at Shelly's age? Was it just the age difference, or was Shelly really a pain in the butt? She folded the sweater and returned it to its drawer. Since she was up, she decided she might as well change. To avoid further interruptions from her sister, though, she closed her door.

What a day! Still, her mom had a job again. That would help a lot, as well as improving her mood. Stephanie began to strip off her Burger Heaven tunic and found herself thinking about Kimberly Cullum again. There was no doubt she'd do her best to embarrass Stephanie at school the next day. But instead of anger, she discovered that she felt envy: it must be wonderful to have so much money without having to do a stroke of work for it. Stephanie examined herself in the full-length mirror on the outside of her closet door. She was attractive enough, she supposed, though losing a pound or two wouldn't hurt. But her hair was a mess. Pulling out the clips, she let it fall loose. Catching the end, she unbraided it. She really ought to wash it, but that would mean staying up at least three more hours till it dried, and she seriously doubted she could manage that. She could have blow-dried it, but it never seemed to come out quite right when she did that. All she needed to finish the day off as a total disaster was to ruin her hair. She'd better wait till the next day. . . . God, she hoped she wasn't getting bags under her eyes!

As she finished changing, she thought about Kimberly again. It must be lovely to be rich, she decided. Kimberly *never* looked anything other than her best. And she didn't have money worries, or hair worries. If only *she* were rich, she'd have no problems. No problems at all . . .

Kimberly carefully parked her bright red BMW by the garden wall and then retrieved her package from the rear seat. David hopped out of the passenger side and hovered over her as she crunched across the gravel pathway to the large front door of her home. He was waiting to see if he was supposed to stay or go home. Kimberly ignored him as she used her key to open the door. Then she barely glanced at him.

"Come in, if you must," she said, entering the house. David followed her in, quietly closing the door behind them.

The fading light outside shone through the stained-glass inserts in the front door, casting long ribbons of colored light across the highly polished oak floor in the entrance hall. There was the faint sound of a television set in the distance—her mother, watching one of those dreary shows she enjoyed. That probably meant her father was in the library, reading or working on another takeover project. Tucking the gift box more firmly under her arm, Kimberly headed for the sun room.

This was probably the most relaxing room in the

whole house. It contained none of the statues and antique vases that adorned the other rooms, and the furniture here was for sitting in, not looking at. The entire outside wall was glass and served as a greenhouse that bulged out onto the rear lawn. Carefully tended plants filled the area and made the room seem like a part of nature. Kimberly sat in one of the three wing chairs. She placed her box on the large teak table beside the chair and removed the lid. David sat quietly in a chair on the opposite side of the table, watching her as she unwrapped the mirror and removed it from the box.

Kimberly felt a faint thrill as she did so. This was definitely a unique piece of craftsmanship, not massproduced garbage. And she had bought it so cheap from that old fool. It fitted nicely into her hand, and she held it up, studying her reflection in the glass. The mirror was flawless and cast back a brilliant image of her beautiful features.

She examined herself with immense satisfaction. She was not merely attractive but refined and wealthy as well. Quite a combination, really. Not at all like that low-class Stephanie Kirk! It had been so satisfying to see her on her hands and knees, scrubbing the floor. That was where someone of her class belonged! It galled Kimberly that she was forced to go to the same school with such nobodies, but her father was inflexible in his refusal to let her transfer to a private school—one that would better suit their status and her sensibilities.

"I pay crippling amounts of taxes into the school

district," he growled. "And you are going to make certain that some of them, at least, are earned. You'll go to a good college when you're done with that place—if your grades warrant it, that is." He was constantly harping on her grades—as if they mattered. She had no intention of ever having to work for a living, no matter what the other kids in her class had to do!

Like that Stephanie Kirk. She was one of the kids who irritated her most. She always got better grades and was more popular than Kimberly. Not that Kimberly cared about being popular, of course, but she resented the attention that Stephanie got. And Stephanie was—in a vulgar sort of way—quite pretty, too. Her blond hair appealed to boys, Kimberly supposed. Especially that rather attractive Scott Berman . . . Kimberly shook the thought from her head. Why, someone might think she was *jealous* of that silly little tramp!

Returning her attention to the mirror, Kimberly frowned slightly. She couldn't quite put her finger on it, but the image in the mirror seemed . . . well, *odd*. Not quite right. She bit her lip, puzzled.

The expression on the image in the mirror didn't change.

A chill ran through Kimberly as she stared at her face. It didn't blink when she did. Then she noticed what else was odd about it.

Her image was wearing a royal blue blouse with gold threads. Kimberly was wearing a deep green silk shirt.

With a startled cry, she dropped the mirror. It fell into her lap, reflecting only the ceiling.

"What's wrong?" David asked, concern and puzzlement in his voice.

"The mirror!" she said, flustered. Could she really have seen a false image? She stopped herself from saying any more. David would think she was crazy if she told him she'd seen a reflection that couldn't exist. She stared at the mirror, wondering what would happen if she peered into it again. Then she felt foolish for being so alarmed by a stupid mirror. Resolutely she snatched it up again and forced herself to stare into it.

She looked back out at herself. And this time the image was wearing the green shirt. . . . The reflection shimmered and changed. It was wearing the blue top once again.

This was definitely eerie. Kimberly's hands were shaking. How could a mirror do that? It had to reflect whatever looked into it! And how could the mirror possibly know that she owned a blue shirt like that?

Trying to stay calm, Kimberly turned the mirror over in her hands. Maybe this was a trick. That old man must have done something, fiddled with the mirror somehow. She didn't know how he could have, but something very strange was happening here. Why was it showing a false reflection?

The back of the mirror was less ornate than the front. The candlestick from the handle continued up the reverse side and around the frame. Etched on the back was an inscription: "This mirror shows what is—and also what is to come."

She read the words three times before their meaning sank in, and then she laughed out loud at the absurdity of the claim.

"What's wrong?" David asked again.

"Don't you ever ask any other question?" she snapped. Then she pointed to the back of the mirror. "According to this, I've just bought a magic mirror!"

"What?" He got up and stood peering over her shoulder at the back of the mirror. His pleasant face was creased by a frown as he read the inscription. "That's dumb," he finally announced.

"Of *course* it's dumb, you idiot," Kimberly snapped. "No one would sell a genuine magic mirror for two hundred dollars—even if such a thing existed. Only—"

"Only what?" asked David, clearly torn between laughing at her and trying to stay on her good side.

"Only I *did* see something strange. . . ." She slowly turned the mirror over again. "The reflection showed me in one of my other blouses." Aware of how silly the claim sounded, she wondered if the mirror would reflect her back normally and make her appear to be a fool. Would that be worse than if it actually changed though? Her fear of looking stupid was washed away as the mirror clouded over and showed her wearing the blue top once more. "It's happening again," she said slowly, as David gasped in shock. "This is beyond weird." She stared into the mirror, unwilling to believe that it really could show the future, but unable to explain what she was seeing. And what David could obviously see, too. It wasn't a trick of the light or her eyes—but what *was* it?

"This is impossible," David muttered, obviously frightened. "You're not wearing that top!"

"I know that," she snapped. "But how is it able to do this? And why?" She stared at her own reflection, wondering if this was all she would see. If this *was* somehow a view into her own future, it was actually rather disappointing. After all, it simply showed her wearing one of her favorite blouses—something she'd obviously do at some time. The initial shock was wearing off when she noticed something else.

Though David was still staring over her shoulder into the mirror, the image was only of her; there was no reflection of David. And her image *was* a mirror image—the part in her hair was slightly left of center in the image, and it was slightly right of center on her head. As she adjusted the mirror slightly, the image changed, but it didn't reflect what she was doing. She held up her right hand, but the hand of the mirror-Kimberly stayed down.

"Bizarre," muttered David. He moved around to face her. "What are you going to do with it?"

"Do?" She hadn't thought about it. "It's *mine*," she said fiercely. "I'll work something out. If it *is* showing me the future, maybe I can learn something useful." She glanced down into the mirror again and then stiffened with shock.

Though David was now standing in front of her, his image had finally appeared in the mirror. She could see over her shoulder that David—also dressed differently now, in jeans and a T-shirt—was creeping up behind her. He held up a large carving knife, which he slashed down at her image's back. His face was twisted in anger and—

"No!" she screamed, jumping up involuntarily, even though she knew there was no one behind her. The mirror fell from her nerveless fingers. As she was starting to realize that she'd dropped a priceless item to the floor, where it would shatter, David's reflexes kicked in. He managed to catch the mirror in midair.

Kimberly fell back a step, staring in horror at her boyfriend. *She had just seen him try to kill her!* It was horrible, unbelievable. . . .

Misunderstanding her cry and expression, David grinned. "It's okay, I caught it," he said, holding the mirror out to her.

"Get away from me!" she screamed, backing up another step.

Puzzled, he stared at her. "Kimberly? What's wrong?"

"Get out of here!" she yelled frantically. All she could see was the flash of the knife blade she had glimpsed in the mirror, and that twisted expression on David's face. "Now! Go!"

"But—"

"Get out!" she screamed, on the verge of hysteria. She glanced around for something to throw at him.

"Okay, okay," he agreed, trying to placate her. "I'm going. No big deal." He shook his head. "I don't know what's gotten into you, but we'll talk about it tomorrow."

"No!" she howled, scared and shaking. "Get out! I never want to see you again!"

"We'll—" he started to say. Then his eyes fastened on some image in the mirror that Kimberly couldn't see. Whatever he saw, though, drained the blood from his face. His hand shook, and the mirror fell from his fingers. Luckily it dropped onto the seat of her chair, not to the hard floor. David swallowed, staring at her with terror in his eyes that matched her own fear. Without another word, he whirled and ran from the room. Seconds later she heard the front door slam shut as he fled from the house.

Alone, Kimberly stared at the mirror. It was lying facedown on the chair, so she saw no further images to haunt her thoughts. But she couldn't drive from her mind that vision of David attacking her.

If the mirror *could* tell the future, then it was telling her that David was going to try to kill her. . . .

# CHAPTER 3

Stephanie brushed furiously at her hair and stared into her mirror, annoyed. She knew she should have washed her hair the night before, and now it was refusing to behave no matter how hard she worked at it. She yanked until it brought tears to her eyes, and still she looked as if she'd spent the night sleeping in a haystack. Muttering under her breath, she started to plait her hair. At least that way it wouldn't look too ugly. . . .

It was the start of another beautiful school day.

She pulled on her jeans and slipped into her shoes while she considered which top to wear. Maybe she should just wear a sack over her whole upper body and be done with it. Finally she settled on her blue sweater. She dragged it on over her braid and rolled up the sleeves. She snatched up her bag, barely remembering to cram the history notes she'd borrowed from Scott into it, and left her room. Then she had to go back for her watch. Should she wear any other jewelry? She stared at her reflection in the mirror and shuddered. There wasn't any point. Nothing could improve how she looked! If only she could stay home and hide away from the world. But her mom would never go for that.

Shelly was already in the kitchen, making inroads on a blueberry muffin. Mom was sipping at her coffee. Dad was still in the bathroom, judging by the off-key singing and the sound of the shower. Stephanie poured herself some juice.

"Is that your entire breakfast?" her mother asked.

"I'm not hungry," Stephanie replied. All she could think about was Kimberly waiting at school to embarrass her. The thought made a knot out of her stomach.

"Pigged out on greasy burgers last night, I'll bet," said Shelly.

"I work there," Stephanie answered. "I don't eat there." She drank her juice and glanced at her watch. Right on cue a car horn sounded outside. "That's Nicki," she said. She gave her mother a quick kiss and a hug. "Bye. Best of luck with the new job."

"Thank you, dear." As Stephanie headed for the door, her mother added, "Eat some lunch! And did you remember Scott's notes?"

"Yes and yes!" Stephanie called back as she shot out the door. She almost tripped over Monty, who was outside, running in circles. She managed to get through the gate without letting him loose, then climbed into Nicki's car. "Hi."

"Hi." Nicki pulled away from the house, accompanied by frantic barking from Monty. Stephanie knew he was firmly convinced he'd scared off an intruder, and he would march proudly back to the house he'd saved from invading barbarians. It would make his day.

Stephanie glanced at her friend. Nicki was immaculate, as always. "You look great," she commented. "I hate you."

Grinning, Nicki tossed a quick glance in Stephanie's direction. "Bad hair day, huh?"

"Bad *everything* day," Stephanie replied. "How come you never have days like this?"

"Because I have a pure spirit," said Nicki solemnly, then burst into a fit of giggles.

"No, seriously," Stephanie said. She couldn't help feeling a little more cheerful, though. Being around Nicki did wonders for her; she had a knack for driving away depression.

"I'm always serious." Nicki stuck her chin in the air in mock anger. "I have a lovely, serene spirit." Then she giggled again. "And did you hear what Josh Beldon said about my body?"

"He's got a dirty mind," Stephanie pointed out. "He's *always* saying things. Why? Are you thinking of going out with him?"

"Not unless I get a black belt in tae kwon do first," replied Nicki. "Speaking of going out, is Scott taking you to Arnold's new film on Friday?" They spent the rest of the trip to school discussing movies.

They had parked and were on their way into school when Stephanie stopped and groaned. "There's Kimberly," she muttered. Now she was in for it. . . .

Kimberly was hurrying toward the building. She looked over at Stephanie and Nicki without reacting and didn't pause. Stephanie stared at her retreating back, puzzled.

"I don't believe it," she said. "That's the first time she hasn't stopped to say something nasty to me. And after last night I was certain she'd start in today."

"Don't knock it," Nicki advised. "Maybe her brain overloaded or something. She'll be back to her Wicked Witch of the West persona by midmorning, you can bet on it." Then she frowned. "Hey, she was alone. I didn't see Blaise anywhere. I thought she kept him on a real short leash."

Stephanie considered this. "Yeah," she agreed. "That *is* weird. She's undressed without her shadow, isn't she?" She glanced around the throng of other students heading for the school. "I don't see David anywhere, either."

"Maybe he's sick," Nicki suggested. "It'd turn *my* stomach to hang around with Kimberly all the time."

Stephanie chuckled at the thought. "It must get pretty rough," she agreed. "But— Oh, there he is." She nodded toward a small knot of students that David was trying to hide behind.

"Come on," said Nicki, moving across to intercept him. Stephanie shrugged and followed. David caught sight of them approaching. For a fleeting second he acted almost terrified of them, but then he managed to regain most of his composure. "Yo, David!" Nicki said firmly. "On your own today?"

"Uh, yes." He tried to move on, but Nicki was blocking his path.

"Slipped your leash, have you?" she asked. When he stared at her blankly, she added, "Not with Kimberly today?"

"No!" he snapped with more force than Stephanie would have imagined him capable of producing. "It's over between us. Finished." Without giving them a chance to comment, he rudely pushed Nicki aside and dashed for the nearest door.

"Wooo," said Nicki. "He's getting physical!" Then she looked at Stephanie. "You think he means it about having split with Kimberly?"

"Why?" Stephanie shot back. "Are you interested in him now?"

"No way!" Nicki frowned. "It's just that I never thought Kimberly would *let* him go."

Stephanie nodded. "I know what you mean. Once she has her hooks in . . . I wonder what happened to them?"

Nicki grinned. "Maybe she tried to get fresh, and he's not that kind of boy?"

Normally Stephanie would have joined in her friend's laughter, but there was something odd about the way David had reacted when Nicki mentioned Kimberly's name. "Did you see his face?" she asked quietly. "He looked as if something had scared him. I wonder what it could be?"

In the men's room David splashed water on his face, trying to calm himself. He'd had a very bad night, filled with horrible visions and nightmares. And those silly girls had brought back most of them. Shaking, he dried his face. His eyes slid up to stare at his reflection: it was a relief to see that it was just a reflection.

Not like last night . . .

He'd been ready to hand the mirror back to Kimberly when he'd seen himself in it—dressed in a T-shirt and jeans. Kimberly was standing over him, wild-eyed and crazy. In her hands she clutched a gun. Blood had pooled at her feet. . . .

*His* blood.

He was stretched out on the floor, a spreading lake of blood around his motionless body.

That damned mirror had shown him his own death! And Kimberly was to be his murderer.

No matter what he did, he couldn't get the image out of his mind. The vision of Kimberly with a gun, staring down at his body. He could almost feel the pain and smell the blood. The images were getting stronger, blanking out all other thoughts. He groaned and clenched his fists. He had to get rid of that image! He *had* to!

Stephanie and Nicki were heading for their lockers when they heard a cheerful cry. Stephanie turned to see Scott weaving a path through the other kids toward them. She waited, a smile on her face, for him to catch up.

Scott was one of the best things that had ever happened to Stephanie. He was a few inches taller than she, and his hair was always an untidy tangle of dark curls that gave him a wild look. In his faded jeans and dark T-shirt he had the appearance of a rebel. Actually, he was nothing of the sort. He was on the baseball team and a straight A student, with glorious brains to match his looks. He did enjoy cultivating the moody, broody appearance, though.

"I hope you've got something for me," he said as he caught up with them.

"You bet," Stephanie replied, while Nicki rolled her eyes. Stretching her neck, she kissed him lightly on the lips.

"That, too," he agreed, kissing her back. "But I *was* referring to my history notes."

"Oh, yeah, right," Nicki said scornfully. "Like we'd believe *that* story."

Scott grinned. "It happens to be true. You've just got a dirty mind."

"So I've been told," Nicki agreed. "Want to check it out?"

"Down, girl," said Stephanie firmly. "He happens to be *my* guy, and there are some things you don't share with your best friend." She searched in her bag and pulled out Scott's notes. "Thanks."

"Some best friend," grumbled Nicki. "Not only

won't you share your boyfriend with me but you won't even ask to borrow *my* notes."

"That's because she wanted to be able to read them," Scott replied, stashing his notes in his backpack. Nicki's handwriting was reputed to be the worst in the school. Stephanie wasn't convinced, but she hadn't found anyone's worse. Scott gave her another quick kiss. "See you Friday?"

"You'd better," she said.

"Wouldn't miss it for the world, and you know it." He grinned at her, winked at Nicki, then headed off down the corridor.

"Why can't I find a guy like that?" complained Nicki. "Mmmm—nice walk."

Stephanie punched her in the arm. *"That's* why," she answered. "You're never serious about anything."

"I am, too! He does have nice—handwriting."

David's attempts to clear his mind had failed utterly. Nothing seemed real to him except the image burning itself into his brain. His bullet-riddled body, the spreading pool of blood, Kimberly with the gun . . . It all refused to go away. Sobbing with fear and frustration, he collapsed into a heap in the corner. He was exhausted and badly needed sleep. But he needed to get rid of that chilling, haunting picture even more.

So lost was he in his personal nightmare that it took a sharp kick to make David aware that he was no longer alone in the men's room. Gasping from pain, he raised his eyes from the corner he was huddled in to see Brent Wardlow and two of his sycophants grinning down at him.

"What have we got here?" sneered Brent, spitting out the match on which he had been chewing. "I think it's something the cat puked up." His two friends sniggered at this. All three were dressed very similarly —Brent set the style, and his mindless friends merely copied him. He wore a faded T-shirt, bleached jeans, and high-tops with the laces undone. Brent's hair was long, hanging over his eyes in front and shaved up level with the tops of his ears in the back. On his hands he wore fingerless gloves, with metal studs set in the leather. When he punched someone, the studs made nasty cuts. And he punched people as often as he could get away with it.

It was starting to sink in to David that he was in very immediate trouble. He tried to get to his feet, but Brent feinted a kick at his face.

"Did I say you could get up?" he asked. "Did I?"

"Leave me alone," David replied, trying not to show how scared he was. It clearly didn't fool Brent for a second. He spat on David's leg.

"You didn't answer my question," he said. "That's rude of you." He grinned at his friends. "Looks like this trash doesn't have any manners, guys."

"Maybe we should teach him a little etiquette?" one of them suggested, cracking his knuckles.

Watching David squirm, Brent pretended to consider this. "Yeah, that sounds like a good idea to me," he agreed. "People gotta know when to show respect." His two friends giggled at the thought. As Brent started to reach down to grab David's shirt, the door opened and Scott walked in.

It didn't take a genius to see what was happening here. Scott's eyes flickered over the trio hovering over David. With a deceptively mild tone, he said, "Lay off him, Brent. Why don't you go get your fun bashing your heads against a wall somewhere?"

Spinning on his heel, Brent scowled at Scott. "Stay outta this," he growled. "Unless you'd like us to take you on instead?"

Scott smiled back at him. "Come off it, Brent. Beating up on somebody helpless is about the limit of your courage and skill." He let his backpack fall to the floor and clenched his fists. "But don't let me stop you if you want to be a jackass."

Brent eyed him warily, making no move to attack. "In case you hadn't noticed, Berman, there's three of us and one of you."

Scott acted mildly surprised. "Gee, I didn't know you could count that high, Brent," he said. "You've been taking extra classes, right?"

"Anyway," added David, seizing his chance to get to his feet now that Brent was no longer looming over him, "it's three against two." He wasn't really a fighter—he'd been beaten up a time or three in the past—but he couldn't let Scott stand alone against Brent and his cronies. He clenched his fists and pretended determination.

Brent checked first one then the other. Even David could see that he didn't care for the odds. But Brent was nasty and stupid enough to refuse to back down for fear that he'd lose respect. At the moment they had a standoff, not a solution.

The bell for first period rang, clattering and raucous. David jumped at the noise.

Brent scowled again. "Looks like we have to postpone this," he announced darkly. He jabbed a finger at Scott. "But I won't forget this, Berman. I'll settle with you."

"Yeah, I'm terrified," agreed Scott gently. He didn't relax his stance until Brent and his friends slammed their way out of the men's room. There was a growl from Brent and a yelp as he pushed someone out of his path. Then the door closed behind him. Scott picked up his pack. "You okay?" he asked David.

Letting his breath out with a giant sigh, David nodded. "Yeah. You stopped them before they really started." There was an ache in his shin where Brent had kicked him, but he'd survived. "Thanks."

"No problem," Scott replied. He scratched at his neck a moment, clearly trying to find the right thing to say. "Look," he finally managed, "if you've got a problem, I'm willing to listen. I can't guarantee good advice, but—"

David shook his head. "No." The image that haunted him returned. "No. There's nothing anybody can help me with." *The roar of the gun, the blood dripping* . . . With a shudder of horror, he wrenched his attention back to Scott. "I'll be okay," he lied. Without giving Scott a chance to question him further, he rushed out into the hall.

He had to concentrate on his work. He couldn't let the image of his own murder prey on his mind like this! He couldn't!

Blindly he stumbled along. There was the stink of blood in his nostrils. His blood—at Kimberly's hands. . . .

# CHAPTER 4

Afraid they were going to be late, Stephanie and Nicki ran through the mall crowds toward Burger Heaven. They had been late being dismissed at school, and then traffic had been slow all the way to the mall. With just a few minutes left before they were to clock in, Stephanie was praying they'd make it in time. All Henry Blake needed was the slightest excuse, and he'd have a field day inventing rotten chores for her to perform. Not that he really needed an excuse—he picked on Stephanie for no reason that she'd been able to discover.

They didn't have time to look at the stores on their way in, but Stephanie did spot Kimberly. The other girl seemed to be heading somewhere in a very agitated state. Stephanie hadn't been able to believe her luck that Kimberly hadn't picked on her at school all day. In fact, she'd seemed completely preoccupied —almost haunted—by some problem of her own. Then Scott had mentioned a very bizarre encounter he'd had with David. Stephanie suspected that all was not well between the pair. But what could possibly have caused them not only to fall out but to freak out as well?

She shrugged mentally. What difference did it make? She wasn't a friend of theirs. And their problems had saved her from more of Kimberly's stinging comments.

Stephanie and Nicki hurried into Burger Heaven with one minute to spare. As they slipped into the staff area, breathing sighs of relief, Blake barred their way. He glared at them both.

"You're late," he accused.

"Not yet," Nicki corrected him. "Move out of the way so we can clock in."

Blake didn't move. "I say you're late," he replied. "Are you arguing with me?"

Nicki glowered at him. "Darn right I am!" she snapped. "If we're late, it'll be because you're stopping us from clocking in. So move."

Stephanie realized that Blake was going to make them late by blocking their way to the time clock. It was mean and petty of him, but that was his style. They could stand and argue with him—and be late— or do something unexpected. "You're probably right," she agreed meekly. Nicki shot her a betrayed look.

"My watch must be slow." Stephanie held up her wrist and shook it. "Yeah, look."

It would have taken someone with far more brains than Blake not to shift forward and squint down at her wrist. Stephanie shot Nicki a quick glance and jerked her head past Blake. Catching on, Nicki grinned and slid past him, snatched up their time cards, and sank them into the time clock. Blake realized he'd been tricked, but he was too slow to stop Nicki.

"What do you know?" said Nicki with a slow drawl. "We're right on time, Steph." She gave the irate Blake an innocent smile. "Did you want to say something, or should we get to work?"

"You're not supposed to stamp another worker's time card," Blake growled.

"Are you trying to say we didn't arrive together?" asked Nicki.

Realizing he couldn't win this argument, Blake abandoned it. Instead, he spun around to Stephanie. "You're on cleanup duty tonight," he snapped.

"It's not her turn," said Nicki indignantly.

"It is if I say it is," Blake replied.

"It's okay," Stephanie said with a sigh. "I guess I'm on cleanup—again." It wasn't worth another argument. Blake had won on this, so he might just leave them alone for the rest of the shift. With a curt nod, he stomped off to find someone else to pick on. Nicki was just about to start in on Stephanie, but Stephanie shook her head. "It's not worth a fight, Nicki. Honest, it really isn't."

Nicki made a rude gesture in the direction Blake

had taken. "I'd really like to see him get what he deserves one of these days."

"He already has," Stephanie answered. "We'll be out of here in a few months and off to college. He'll be here forever. I can't think of a worse punishment, can you?"

"Yes," replied Nicki with a nasty little smile. "Your problem is a lack of imagination. Fortunately I'm not so limited. I'd take one of those big metal spatulas, heat it up on the biggest burner and then—" She made a poking motion. "Right up as far as it would go."

Stephanie smiled. There was a certain temptation in the idea. . . . Then she shook her head and gathered up her supplies. It was going to be another long, tough shift.

Kimberly paused outside the dingy antique shop, suffering from serious second thoughts. Maybe she was just asking for trouble. But she had to know! Pushing the door open, she plunged into the stench of mold and dust and stale coffee. The store was just as dark and unpleasant as it had been the previous night. Nothing seemed to have been sold, which didn't surprise her.

There was the sound of movement from the back room, and then Dolman emerged. His eyes narrowed when he saw who it was. "Come for another bargain?" he asked.

"No." Kimberly shifted uneasily from foot to foot. "I want to ask you about that mirror."

He snorted, then scratched his dirty nose. "What about it?"

"Is—" She faltered, losing her resolve. Seeing his unpleasant expression, she took a deep breath and forced herself to ask. "Is there something special about that mirror?"

"You mean aside from the fact that you bought it for a ridiculously low price?" grumbled Dolman. "No. What could there be?"

Her hopes fell, even though she'd been expecting that reply. It was too late to back out now, even if she did look like a fool. "The inscription on the back says that the mirror can show what's going to happen."

"Really?" Dolman didn't sound surprised by the news. "Well, I'm afraid I can't guarantee that. Magic mirrors went out with Sleeping Beauty."

Kimberly felt her skin flush with embarrassment. Despite this, she refused to back down. She was almost certain that Dolman knew what she was talking about and was just playing games with her. "I saw something odd in the mirror," she persisted. "It didn't reflect me as I was."

Dolman shrugged. "Maybe you looked at it wrong. Mirrors can be funny about what they show sometimes."

"It showed me in different clothes," snapped Kimberly.

"Really?" Dolman was working at pretending to be wide-eyed and innocent. "And did it show you in a flattering outfit?"

"You're making fun of me," she replied.

"What do you expect?" he countered. "Magic mirrors! Different reflections! Something terrible happening to you." He threw up his hands in disgust. "Utter nonsense!"

Kimberly glared at him. "I didn't say it showed anything bad happening to me," she said triumphantly.

"Well, it doesn't take a genius to figure it out," he snapped back. "If it had been something good, you wouldn't have come back, would you?"

Her hopes were dashed again. Miserably, Kimberly wrung her hands. He did have logic on his side—her story sounded very foolish. But she was still convinced that he was putting on an act. That he *knew* she'd really seen something—and that he had no intention of admitting it. "Do those images have to come true?" she demanded. "Does the mirror show what *will* happen or what *might* happen?"

Dolman shook his head. The wisps of thin white hair fluttered. "Mirrors reflect back whatever is in front of them," he replied. "If you see anything else, then you must be on something." He sniffed loudly. "You young people are all alike. Probably doing drugs or drinking." He moved closer and sniffed again. "Can't tell, with all that perfume you're wearing. Trying to hide the telltale smell?"

"You filthy little wretch," Kimberly said hotly. "I don't touch drugs—or alcohol."

He shrugged. "Well, if you're seeing things without their help, maybe you should start on them. They might get rid of your hallucinations."

Kimberly was caught between anger and hopelessness. It was clear that she wasn't going to get anywhere with Dolman. Yet she was sure that he knew more than he was telling, even if he wouldn't admit it. Despite his denials, she was certain that the mirror showed the future. But was it what *would* happen or what *could* happen? "Tell me!" she cried. "Does it have to happen?"

"Get out," he told her. "Or I'll send for a security guard and have you thrown out."

Furious, she spun around and stormed for the door. Then she paused and glared back at him. "You'll pay for this," she told him. "I'll make sure of it. You'll pay." Then she stalked out.

Dolman watched her go, a smile tugging at his lips. "Oh, no," he said softly. *"You'll* pay for it. With your life . . ."

Stephanie was hauling stinking garbage bags out to the Dumpster behind Burger Heaven. Ketchup and bits of food were stuck to her sleeve and under her nails. This was the filthiest part of the job, and Blake had inflicted it on her to punish her. She hated it, but there wasn't anything she could do about it. She just had to avoid touching her hair with her hands. All she needed was sauce in her hair!

As she was dragging the next bag to the green monstrosity of a Dumpster, Stephanie was startled to see a familiar figure pacing the authorized-personnel-only area. It was Kimberly Cullum. Instead of her usual haughty stride, though, she was stumbling back and forth, her shoulders hunched, her face red. She looked as if she'd been crying. Despite the fact that she didn't care for Kimberly, Stephanie was too kind to pretend she didn't notice the other girl. She called out to her.

Kimberly stopped and glanced around. She appeared to be dazed and had to struggle to focus her eyes on Stephanie. Then she sighed. "Kirk. Yeah. I came out here to be alone."

"What's wrong, Kimberly?" asked Stephanie. "You look"—she searched for a word that wouldn't be insulting—"lost."

"I *feel* lost," Kimberly admitted honestly. "But what do you care?"

Stephanie bit at her lower lip. "I hate to see anyone as miserable as you are," she replied. "I know we aren't friends, but if I can help at all . . ."

"No," Kimberly answered, but without any anger. Without any hope, either. Then she paused. "You work there," she said.

"Yeah." Stephanie shrugged. "If you can call this work. Living hell is more like it."

"You don't know what hell is!" There was fire in Kimberly's voice, and Stephanie flinched. Then Kimberly calmed down a little. "Do you know that little antique shop in the mall?" she asked.

Stephanie had to think. "The dirty little place? I guess so. Why?"

"I bought a mirror there from a filthy old man who runs it," Kimberly admitted. "I think there's something wrong with it."

Puzzled, Stephanie asked, "Won't he give you a refund?"

"Not that sort of wrong." She shook her head. *"Wrong.* Evil. It showed me—" She shuddered. Then she seemed to realize what she had been saying. Her eyes narrowed suspiciously. "What do you care, anyway? You're just trying to get me to say something so you can make fun of me. That's all!"

"That's not true," Stephanie protested, hurt by the accusation. "I was only trying to help."

"Like hell you were." Kimberly acted as if she wanted to bite or claw. "I know you, Kirk—you're just *hoping* to see me murdered, aren't you? You'd like that, wouldn't you? Well, it isn't going to happen! It isn't!" Spinning around, Kimberly stormed away.

Bewildered, Stephanie simply stared after the other girl. She had no idea what that was all about. Kimberly had seemed to be having a nervous breakdown. Maybe she was coming unhinged.

From the doorway behind her, Blake snapped, "You're paid to *work,* not to laze around and talk."

Ouch. Just what she needed. Meekly she turned to see a glowering Blake. "Sorry," she said. "I'm almost done."

"Don't let me catch you goofing off again!" he yelled. "Unless you want to be fired." He stared at her. *"Is* that what you want?"

She shook her head. "I'll be finished soon."

"See that you are." Blake stomped back inside.

Stephanie saw Paka there staring indignantly at the

supervisor. Then the girl stepped outside to her. "Stephanie," she muttered, "you have *got* to stand up for yourself. He's walking all over you."

"It's not important," Stephanie replied, heaving the plastic bag of garbage into the Dumpster.

"It *is* important," Paka answered. "If you don't insist that people respect you, you'll never have any dignity. Do you *like* being a doormat?"

"I've got to get this job finished," Stephanie replied. "I can't talk now." She didn't want to argue with her friend. It wouldn't get her anywhere.

Paka shook her head. "You *do* have problems, Stephanie," she said. "But if you won't do anything about them, you'll have to live with what happens." She went back inside.

After pulling another smelly bag from the hallway, Stephanie started back to the Dumpster again. Paka was probably right, she reflected. She *was* a doormat. But she hated to cause more trouble. Was it so bad to try to smooth things over instead of fighting for her rights? As she struggled with the bag, Stephanie wished she didn't need the job so badly. If only she didn't need the money! If she were only more like Kimberly—wealthy, with no cares . . .

She broke off that thought. If there was one thing she could be certain of, it was that Kimberly had far more serious problems than she did right then. Money was obviously not the answer to whatever was troubling Kimberly. She wondered what could be preying on the rich girl's mind. Then she shrugged. What difference did it make? Whatever was bothering her, she'd told Stephanie to butt out. It was none of her business. It had nothing at all to do with her. . . .

With a scream, Kimberly sat up in bed. She was shaking violently, her throat was dry, and her heart was pounding in her ears. For a second she didn't know where she was, and then she realized she was in her bed. Silver light was flowing in through her windows, casting a spectral glow around the room. For just one heart-stopping second, she thought she could see David in the room with her, ready to strike. Then she realized it was nothing more than her cast-off clothes draped over the back of a chair.

She had been in the clutches of another nightmare in which David attacked her. Wielding a huge knife, he had slashed her, grinning savagely as he struck.

Shuddering, she tried to compose herself. It was only a dream—a bad dream. That was all. The same bad dream she'd had the night before. The same violent images of David gleefully hacking into her with a knife. The same terrible, sharp pains that made her sit up, screaming, too terrified to fall asleep again.

Her distress over the mirror was affecting her badly, she knew. Her face was puffy and swollen. Her appetite was completely gone. Her eyes were bloodshot, her ability to concentrate nonexistent. Her nerves were frayed almost to the point of snapping. If something wasn't done, she'd go completely crazy. It was a wonder her mind hadn't snapped by now. Every time she closed her eyes, she could see David with the knife.

Ever since she'd seen the reflection in that mirror.

She glanced nervously at her vanity. The looking glass lay there facedown, as it had for two days. She didn't dare peek into it again. What might it show her the next time?

But how long could this go on? Something had to give soon, and she was terribly afraid it would be her sanity. She *had* to know!

She threw back the covers and slipped out of bed. She smoothed down her silk nightgown; it was wet with her sweat. Hardly caring, she walked slowly across to the vanity, her eyes focused on the hand mirror. In the silver moonlight it seemed almost alive somehow, as if the fairy figure on the frame had twisted about to watch her. She knew it was only her imagination, but she could smell a stench of evil coming from the mirror.

Standing beside it, she hesitated. Then, summoning all her remaining courage and resolve, she snatched up the mirror and held it in front of her face. She held her breath, hardly daring to focus on the reflection. But it was just her own scared face peering back at her.

Yech! She looked terrible! Swollen, red-rimmed eyes, and pale blotchy skin . . .

As she stared at her reflection, she suddenly became aware that it wasn't quite right. Her hand began to shake as she tilted the mirror slightly to take in her neck.

There was a long, jagged cut across the neck of her reflection, from ear to ear. Blood was trickling out of the cut as if there was none left in her body. The reason for the pallor of her skin was now evident.

With a gasp she threw the mirror aside as hard as she could. It slammed into the wall and shattered into a million pieces, showering down onto the carpet. The effort of throwing it had overbalanced her, and she fell to the thick carpet. In the faint moonlight, she saw the tiny glittering shards of the mirror. She pushed herself up on one elbow, staring raptly at the shattered wreckage.

What had happened to the mirror? How could the metal have broken as well as the glass?

For some reason this scared her more than anything else had so far. The entire mirror had broken apart and lay in sparkling fragments on the carpet. At least it would show her no more terrible images! She couldn't take any more.

After a while she managed to draw some strength into her body. Slowly, painfully she sat up, her hand flying to her throat as if to check that it was still intact. Her skin was smooth, and she sighed with relief. She was still alive. But for how long? The image of David coming for her with the knife was burned into her brain. She was utterly certain that it would happen. The mirror had shown her what David intended to do—but not when he would strike. And she had seen herself dead, her throat cut. But was it inevitable? Or could she escape that gruesome fate?

There was one thing she could do. In the mirror she

had seen herself wearing her royal blue blouse with the gold threads. She'd avoided even looking at it in her closet since then. If she didn't wear it, she couldn't be in danger. But if she wore it— How long, though, could she go on like this, waking in terror, living in fear, waiting for David to attack her? Wouldn't it be better to get it over with? To be ready for her fate—and be prepared to defeat it?

She almost had to crawl back to her bed. She was too weak from terror and lack of food for the past two days. But when she reached it, her mind was made up.

In the morning she'd wear the blue blouse. Whatever was going to happen, she'd be ready and waiting. David would not find her an easy or willing victim.

# CHAPTER
# 5

Stephanie helped herself to a handful of grapes and a glass of orange juice. "So," she asked her mother, "how's the job going?"

Mrs. Kirk raised her eyes from the papers she was reading at the breakfast table and sipped at her coffee before replying. "Very well," she said, obviously wanting to return to her notes. "Everybody in my department is creative and pleasant. I think it'll work out fine." She smiled. "And the money will certainly help out. Shelly's already planning on spending my first month's check on new clothes!"

"Typical," Stephanie muttered.

"Well," her mother argued, "things have been kind

of rough for a while. And she *does* need some new things."

"I guess," agreed Stephanie. "But the main thing is that you like your job." *Unlike me,* she added mentally.

"Um, yes." Her mother went back to glancing through her notes.

Stephanie smiled. It was good to see her mother happy again. Being out of work for so long had made her miserable and less confident about herself. Now she was back to her old self, and that made Stephanie feel better, too. She gave her mother a quick kiss on the forehead as she left the kitchen, munching on the last of the grapes. Grabbing her bag, she swung it over her shoulder, gave Monty a quick scratch on the back of his head, and went outside to wait for Nicki.

It was already bright and pleasant. Stephanie smiled. A good day at last!

David leaned forward, clutching the edge of the sink for support. He tried to breathe slowly and evenly, to calm down, but it was no use. He'd suffered through another nightmare-filled night, and he was so tired that he could hardly see straight. There was a haze in his brain, as if his head were wrapped in gauze. Everything was distant and unreal, except the images of Kimberly shooting him. It was the only thought he could focus on, the only island in a sea of insanity. He splashed more water on his face and then toweled it off. The cold water made no difference. Through the roaring in his ears and the haze across his eyes, he could still see and hear only Kimberly and the gun.

He couldn't go on like this. Every second was pure torture. He had to do something. . . . After finishing his ablutions, he managed to stagger into his room and get dressed. He stared at the clock for several minutes before being able to make out the time. He was going to be late for school, but that hardly mattered. Grades were of little interest to him now. All he could focus on was staying alive.

He didn't know if his fate was carved in stone or whether he could change it. But he had to try at least. There was no way he was going to wait meekly for Kimberly to murder him. He knew of only one thing he could do. . . .

Walking into the kitchen, he crossed to the counter by the stove. There, in a block of wood, his mother kept her best carving knives. Without conscious thought, he wrapped his fingers around one of them. With a wrench, he tore it free from the block and slipped it into his backpack. Slinging the pack over his shoulder, he left the house through the back door.

It was time to do or die. One way or another this nightmare was going to be over very soon.

Stephanie and Nicki walked from the parking lot toward school. Nicki was chattering away about some inane comedy show she'd seen on TV the previous night. Stephanie barely paid attention. She glanced around, hoping to catch sight of Scott. He had promised to meet her after work at the mall that night, and she was looking forward to seeing him. It seemed like forever since they'd last spent any time alone together.

She didn't see Scott, but she did spot Kimberly moving slowly across the lot. She seemed more depressed than she had two days earlier. "There's Kimberly," she said.

Nicki stopped talking in midflow and made a face. "She looks *awful,*" she observed. "Serves her right. Money can't buy happiness."

"You've been reading too many fortune cookies," Stephanie told her. "Don't you feel sorry at all for her?"

After a moment's thought, Nicki shook her head. "Not a bit," she admitted cheerfully. "Tell you what —let's go over and make her feel even worse by telling her she's gained a few pounds."

"Actually, she looks kind of skinny."

"Yeah, but we don't have to tell *her* that." Nicki grinned wickedly. "I just *adore* the thought of winding her up. Don't you?"

Stephanie was fairly sure Nicki was joking, though it was difficult to be certain. She wondered about her own feelings. Though Kimberly had never been friendly, it was terrible to see her so miserable. "Just try to be nice to her, will you?" she asked Nicki.

"You know what your trouble is?" asked Nicki. "You're too nice to everyone. Don't you ever get mad and curse and spit like a normal person?"

"That's normal?" Stephanie responded. By now they had almost reached Kimberly. Stephanie called her name out twice before it penetrated the other girl's gloom. "Are you okay?" Stephanie asked her.

"Yeah," added Nicki. "You look like death warmed over. And not too warm." Stephanie was tempted to kick her.

The remark didn't seem to bother Kimberly, which in itself was sort of scary. Her temper was normally on a very short fuse. Now, however, she just shrugged slightly.

"Hi," she muttered vaguely and kept on walking.

Nicki stared after her. "How do you like that?" she demanded, irritated. "We try to be nice and she acts like we don't even exist."

"That was *nice?*" Stephanie asked.

Nicki grinned again. "You don't know what I was *thinking* of saying to her."

"Which is probably a good thing," Stephanie decided. She glanced after Kimberly again, still feeling bad for her.

Nicki pointed to their left. "Stop feeling so sorry for her," she commented. "Here comes her main squeeze. She and David probably just had a row about who should tip the waiter at dinner or something. They'll make up now, and everything will be back to normal. Nauseating." She grimaced.

David was hurrying across to meet Kimberly. He

did look eager to see her, Stephanie realized. Maybe they were going to make up. It was about time. Their problem couldn't have been all that serious. As Stephanie watched, David pulled something from his backpack, then flung the pack aside.

She gasped as she saw the glint of sunlight on steel. *He had a knife!* "Oh, God," she whispered, shocked. Then as loud as she could she screamed, "Kimberly!"

Kimberly spun around and saw David rushing at her with a knife clenched in his upraised fist. Strangely, she didn't appear to be surprised or scared. Stephanie was frozen in place, her scream still echoing in her head. Everything seemed to be happening in slow motion. She felt Nicki grab her arm as several other students screamed. Sunlight danced off the point of the knife as David howled and lunged toward Kimberly.

Then all at once there was something dull and black in Kimberly's fist as she let her own bag drop. Kimberly's hand came up, and the gun in it spat fire again and again. David staggered as the bullets ripped into him, showering blood from the instant wounds in his chest. Then, finally, he collapsed backward, the knife clattering to the pavement as he dropped it.

Nicki started to run toward Kimberly. Stephanie was still in shock from what she had witnessed, but she dimly realized that Kimberly had deliberately gunned down David, and she still held the gun. Nicki was running right into trouble! Stephanie's feet started moving of their own accord. She could hear the other kids scream as they moved away from the scene, which was a far smarter idea.

Even though David was on the ground, Kimberly hadn't finished. Stepping in closer, she fired twice more into his bleeding body. By that time Nicki was behind her. Stephanie had never seen her friend do anything like this before and couldn't imagine what could have possessed her to act like this now. Nicki slammed into Kimberly with her shoulder from behind. The other girl went reeling, her hands outspread to take the impact as she slammed onto the ground. She gave a cry, and then a second one as Nicki stamped down hard on her hand. Stephanie was pretty certain she heard the snap of bones over the sound of Kimberly's scream. Nicki bent down and scooped up the revolver from Kimberly's shattered hand, then pushed the hair away from her eyes.

Seeing that Nicki was fine and Kimberly was disarmed, Stephanie fell to her knees beside David. She felt a sudden pain in both legs, and she knew she'd cut herself and ruined another pair of pantyhose, but that didn't matter right then. She stared down at David's chest trying not to focus on the gaping wounds clearly visible through his T-shirt. Carefully she grabbed his wrist, feeling for a pulse. It was faint and fast. It was hard to think coherently, so she focused on what should be done first—prepare for mouth-to-mouth resuscitation in case he needed it, and try to stop the bleeding.

The knife he'd been carrying lay on the ground beside him. She snatched it up and used it to slash off the hem of her skirt. She needed the material for a bandage, to stop the blood that was gushing from his wounds.

David gave a choked cry, spit up blood, and then nothing.

Stricken, Stephanie grabbed his wrist again, knowing what she'd find. The pulse was gone. "No," she whispered.

His chest was a mess, and blood soaked the ground where he lay. His eyes were open and staring, and blood trickled out of his mouth.

Hands grabbed at her, trying to pull her away. She shook herself free, but the hands returned, more firmly this time, dragging her off David. Stunned, confused, she gazed up at Nicki.

"It's no use," Nicki told her gently but firmly. "He's dead."

"He can't be dead," Stephanie said, shaking her head. "He can't be."

"Believe me," Nicki said. "He's dead."

"Oh, God," muttered Stephanie, staring down at him. She shook her head and allowed Nicki to push her back into a sitting position beside his body. Stephanie started to push her hair out of her eyes and then froze as she saw that her hands were all bloody. It didn't register for a second and then she realized it was David's blood. She'd gotten it on her when she tried to help him.

She started to shake as the reality of what she'd been through hit her. Kimberly was sitting on the other side of the body, clutching her hand and crying. "Why?" asked Stephanie, dazed and nauseated. "Why did you do it?"

Kimberly stared back and wiped at her eyes and nose with her good hand. "It was him or me," she said in a far-off voice. "Him or me. And it wasn't going to be me."

Nicki shook her head in disgust. "She's gone crazy. They both must have." She was avoiding the sight of David's body, Stephanie realized. She didn't blame her friend. But she found it difficult to look away. Only a few moments earlier he'd been alive, one of her classmates. Now he was dead, his blood slowly staining the ground.

She became vaguely aware that other people were approaching. One of the teachers—she couldn't remember his name at the moment—swam into view. "What's happened?" he asked in a strange, shrill voice.

"Guess," muttered Nicki in disgust.

Stephanie tried to tell her friend that she shouldn't be so rude to a teacher, but she found it impossible to concentrate. She heard a ringing in her ears, and the sky was spinning above her. All she could see was a bright blur. All she could smell was the coppery stench of blood. All she could hear above the ringing was Nicki's urgent voice. After that, nothing.

\* \* \*

When she woke again, she was lying down. The unmistakable smell of a hospital made her want to gag, and she opened her eyes. When her eyes finally focused, she saw that she was in a small cubicle with an off-white ceiling, and Nicki was bending over her.

"What happened?" she asked, puzzled. She felt a little light-headed, but not much else.

"You fainted," Nicki answered. "Out like a light."

Then it all came back in a stampede of images. Kimberly gunning David down, David and the knife, his blood on her hands . . . She sat up and realized she was on a stretcher in the emergency room. Outside the open door were several nurses and two police officers. One of them she recognized—Mr. Powers, Nicki's father. They were talking. Beyond them she could see doctors and other nurses moving about purposefully.

"David," she said slowly.

"He's dead," replied Nicki bluntly. "Five bullets."

Stephanie shuddered. She glanced at her hands, but they were clean now. Someone must have washed his blood off them. Trying to fight back the shock and confusion, she asked: "Kimberly?"

"She's in the next room." Nicki grimaced. "I broke her hand when I stomped on it."

Remembering Nicki's crazy actions, Stephanie grabbed her friend's hand. "Why did you do such a stupid thing?"

Shrugging, Nicki acted almost embarrassed. "I guess it's a genetic thing. Both my parents are cops.

All I could think was that Kimberly had gone mad and had a gun. She could have shot somebody else next. My folks taught me how to protect myself, and I just felt that I had to stop her. She was crazy enough to keep on shooting."

Stephanie shook her head slowly. She was having difficult assimilating this. "And now what?" she asked.

"Well, the butchers here have checked you out," Nicki told her. "They've decided that there's no money to be made out of treating you, so you'll be allowed to go home when your mom arrives to collect you." Nicki gave a slight smile. "Trying to help David was good, Steph. I guess it shows the difference between us, doesn't it? You try to help, while I stomp the crap out of someone."

That was the old Nicki again, taking nothing seriously. Stephanie wondered if Nicki was as shocked by David's killing as she was. It was hard to tell. She constantly tried to treat everything as a joke. But when action was needed, Nicki had proven she was the first one to act. "What about Kimberly?" she asked.

"She'll never play the violin again," Nicki replied.

"I meant—"

"I *know* what you meant." Nicki sighed. "She's under arrest, of course. For murdering David Blaise."

Stephanie had been more than half expecting that news, but it was still a shock. One of her—well, not *friends*, but at least a classmate—arrested for the murder of another. Her boyfriend, even! Shaking her head, she said, "But he attacked her. She was acting in self-defense. You saw that."

Nicki nodded. "Yes, but *she* was carrying a gun in her bag. That makes it seem as if they were both planning murder, doesn't it?" Stephanie couldn't think of anything to say to that. Nicki sighed again. "Bummer of a start to the day, isn't it?"

# CHAPTER
# 6

~≈~

Stephanie's mother insisted on her going straight to bed when they arrived home, despite all of Stephanie's protests. "You've had a dreadful shock," she said firmly. "You need rest—and chicken soup."

Wincing at the thought, Stephanie said, "I'm fine and I'm not hungry."

"Don't argue, young lady," her mother insisted, pushing her toward her room. "You don't eat properly. I'm not surprised you fainted."

"Working in Burger Heaven can really put you off food," Stephanie muttered, but she gave in and headed for her room. By the time she was changed and sitting up in bed, her mother was back with a bowl of steaming chicken noodle soup.

"And I'm going to sit here while you eat this," Mrs. Kirk told her. "Get it down, or else."

Despite her protests, Stephanie discovered that she did have an appetite, and it didn't take her long to finish the soup. Her mother beamed at her and then left her to her thoughts. As she lay back on her bed, Stephanie stared at the ceiling, trying to clear her mind of the images that were haunting her.

She was numb to most of the emotional aspects of the shooting. She winced as she remembered the gun going off and the blood all over her and the pavement, but she felt no real sense of loss at David's death. She wondered if she was so callous that the death of another human being meant little to her or whether the numbness was simply an aftereffect of shock. The problem was that she had never really known David. He had been a quiet sort of guy who was always there in the background, kind of good-looking, but not her type. He'd been shy and passive, which had made him a natural target for any bullies. She remembered Scott mentioning that Brent Wardlow had been picking on David. And even though Kimberly had been dating David for some months, Stephanie suspected that there was never any strong emotional bond of love or even affection between them. Kimberly apparently liked having David around because she wanted a good-looking boyfriend as an ornament and because he'd done whatever she told him to do. He'd seemed to be more like a puppy dog than a human being to her.

So what on earth could have changed that? If Kimberly hadn't felt any strong affection for David, why had she suddenly developed such a strong hatred for him that would make her carry a gun? And why had David—the quietest boy in school—suddenly gone berserk and attacked Kimberly with a carving knife?

There had been some tension between the pair for a couple days, Stephanie realized. Ever since that night when Kimberly had mocked Stephanie at the mall. She and David had been together then, acting like their old selves. Then, the next day at school, they had avoided each other, and their relationship had taken a nosedive from there. Something must have happened at the mall. . . .

The mall! Stephanie recalled her bizarre conversation with Kimberly behind Burger Heaven. She'd spoken about a mirror she'd bought at that old man's antique store—Dolman's, that was it. Stephanie frowned. She'd passed the dingy little place a few times, of course, but she'd never gone in. Besides, what could have happened there that could have caused that day's tragedy?

The door to her room burst open, and Shelly rushed in, tossing her school bag into her room across the hall as she did. For once, her younger sister acted glad to see Stephanie.

"Way cool!" she exclaimed. "It's all around school that you were there when David Blaise got blown away. What was it like?"

Stephanie stared at Shelly, appalled. "It wasn't *fun!*" she exclaimed. "It was horrible!"

"Yeah, right," her sister agreed, flopping down on the bed. "So tell me all the gruesome details."

"You are sick," Stephanie said, disgusted. "This isn't some kind of game. A person was *killed*. He died right in front of me."

"Neat," Shelly commented, not at all concerned about Stephanie's feelings. "Was there a lot of blood?"

Shocked by her sister's insensitivity, Stephanie glowered at Shelly. "Out," she said coldly. "Right now. Or you'll personally discover how much blood there is when someone's murdered."

Pretending to be hurt, Shelly hopped to her feet. "I only *asked.*"

"The wrong thing," Stephanie snapped. "Get lost, you creep."

Shelly stuck her tongue out, then slammed the door as she left the room.

Stephanie couldn't understand her sister's reaction. Shelly was treating the murder as if it were exciting, not the tragic end to a young man's life. How could anyone be so callous? Her reaction bothered Stephanie almost as much as the killing had. She was still trying to understand it all when Nicki arrived.

"How you doing?" she asked, sitting down on the bed beside Stephanie with a long sigh of relief. She kicked off her shoes, then sat cross-legged.

"Okay, I guess," Stephanie replied. She decided not to mention what had been disturbing her. "So what's the news? Anything happen since I left the hospital?"

"Yeah, tons of stuff." Nicki grimaced. "Dad had a long talk with me, and I managed to squeeze some information out of him. Then Mom had a longer talk with me, and I barely escaped getting my first spanking since I was three. I figured they'd tell me how amazing I was to have taken out Kimberly like that. Instead, my mom almost skinned me." She shrugged. "Parents! Who can figure them out?"

"They were probably scared for you," Stephanie suggested.

"Right, take their side." Nicki wrinkled her nose in disgust. "Typical."

Patting her friend's hand, Stephanie told her, "Well, I thought you were incredibly brave. And dumb."

Nicki grinned. "Trust you to qualify your praise." But she didn't seem upset any longer. "Anyway, while my dad thought he was telling me off, I pumped him for information. Kimberly's suffering from verbal diarrhea, by the sound of things. I think she's trying for an insanity plea."

"What do you mean?"

"Well," said Nicki, settling in for a long story, "at the hospital my dad and his partner did the usual Miranda thing—read her her rights, told her she could have a lawyer with her while she gave her statement and all that. She didn't care and started

80

talking almost faster than they could tape. She claims that she had this magic mirror that showed her the future!" Nicki rolled her eyes. "Like, she couldn't think of any better excuse? Well, she says that she saw in the mirror that David was going to kill her, so she decided to get him first. That's why she stole one of her father's guns and put it in her bag. When David went for her, she was ready." She wrinkled her nose. "The whole thing sucks, doesn't it? She's obviously trying to convince the cops that she's wacko."

Stephanie wasn't so certain. "What about this mirror?" she asked.

"What about it?" Nicki was puzzled.

"Well, couldn't she show it to them?" asked Stephanie. "I mean, if it's supposed to be magic, couldn't she prove it?"

"Get real!" Nicki said incredulously. "A magic mirror! Give me a break! You sure you didn't bang your head too hard on the ground or something? Maybe all your brains bled out?"

Stephanie flushed. "I didn't say I believed it," she snapped, embarrassed. "But *she* might believe it."

Nicki shrugged. "Yeah, and she probably believes in the Easter Bunny, too. That girl is seriously mental, Steph. Anyway, she says she threw the mirror at the wall in a fit of temper, and it's completely broken." She snorted in derision. "Convenient, eh?" Then she stared at her friend and frowned. "What's with you, Steph?" she asked. "You're starting to worry me. You look as if you think there's some truth in all this crap. Are you sure you're okay?"

"Yeah." Stephanie twisted a long strand of her hair around her finger. "It's just that I saw Kimberly behind Burger Heaven the other night. She was really worried and acting strange, and she mentioned that antique store at the mall. You know, Dolman's?"

"That dump?" Nicki shrugged. "So what?"

"Well, I was just thinking before you came that this problem between her and David only dates back a few days. Remember that night she made fun of me when I was cleaning the floor?"

"Yeah. So?"

"Well, she split with David right after that."

Nicki snorted again. "Maybe she saw him checking out your legs or something. That would have ticked her off."

"No, it had to be more serious than that," Stephanie argued.

"He was looking up your skirt?" Nicki suggested.

"Will you be serious?" snapped Stephanie.

"Serious?" Nicki laughed. "Come on, Steph! Kimberly's talking about magic mirrors and seeing the future, and you want me to take it *seriously?*" She made a show of looking around the room. "You aren't going to be the next one with a gun in your bag, are you? Is this an attempt to work up an insanity defense when you go on a crime spree?"

Her friend's joking was getting to Stephanie, like

cloth rubbing on an open wound. "Will you *please* listen to me?" she snapped.

Nicki became really concerned. "Yeah, I'm sorry. It was a hell of a shock having David die on you like that. I don't mean to be so sarcastic. But please—don't start weirding out on me."

"Okay. No more mirror talk." Stephanie was pleased by Nicki's response. She really did care. "Did Kimberly say anything else to the police?"

"Nah. Her filthy rich father arrived right then with an even filthier rich lawyer, and they made her clam up. Dad says they're taking her to jail after her hand's treated." Nicki suddenly blushed. "And then I got yelled out because the stupid lawyer threatened to sue me for breaking Kimberly's hand."

"Really?"

Nicki shrugged. "It's just the usual lawyer response, but it got to my dad. Like I was supposed to just *ask* her to give me the gun?"

"Don't worry about it," Stephanie said. "You're probably right. The lawyer just wanted to get Kimberly off the hook. They all do things like that."

"Yeah, I know." Nicki shifted uncomfortably. "But Dad's using it as an excuse to keep me in line, I guess. I think you're probably right. He and Mom were really scared for me."

Stephanie nodded. She'd been scared for Nicki, too. "And what happens to Kimberly immediately?" she asked.

"They're going to get a shrink to check her out to see if her mental wires are really crossed or if she's faking it. Her father is flying in a specialist from New York. Meanwhile, they've got her on a suicide watch."

"Suicide?" Stephanie blinked. "Do they really think she's likely to kill herself?"

"Nobody thought it was likely she'd kill David," Nicki pointed out. "Anyway, it's standard procedure in these cases. A lot of people who kill for passion regret what they've done and try to make up for it by killing themselves afterward."

Stephanie shuddered. "It's all so horrible, isn't it?" She couldn't have imagined that something like this would ever happen in her quiet little town and that it would involve her and Nicki.

"Life goes on," Nicki replied. "Speaking of which, if I want *my* life to go on, I've got to get to work."

Stephanie had completely forgotten about her job! "I'd better—" she began.

"You'd better stay right there," Nicki told her firmly. "You're taking a sick day. Doctor's orders." She grinned. "I'll break the news to Blake. He'll have to find someone else to carry out the trash tonight."

Stephanie couldn't help feeling bad—and at the same time relieved—about missing work. Though she tried to put a good face on it, Blake was really wearing on her nerves. A day away from him would certainly be welcome! After Nicki left, she was undisturbed until her father arrived home from work. She spent the quiet time trying to put her thoughts in order, but didn't get anywhere.

That story of Kimberly's sounded strained, to say the least. Nicki was right—it was like a fairy tale. A mirror that showed the future, then was conveniently broken before it could be checked out.

But . . .

*Something* had driven Kimberly to murder—and David to his death while trying to kill her. The mirror story might be incredible, but it was the only excuse Kimberly was offering. Stephanie couldn't actually bring herself to believe it, but then she recalled that odd conversation she'd had with the troubled girl. It seemed to tie Dolman into the picture somehow. But how? And was it really any of her concern? Surely the murder would be thoroughly investigated by the police.

Despite everything, she couldn't help feeling sorry for Kimberly. Okay, she was an obnoxious snob, but it was hard to remember that only the day before, Stephanie had been feeling envious of her. And now . . . how things had changed! Something horrible must have been eating at Kimberly to make her do what she'd done.

These thoughts, mixed with images of David's death, were whirling around in her head when her father knocked on the door and peered in. Stephanie smiled at his expression of concern. "I feel fine, Dad," she told him before he could ask the obvious question.

He came over to sit beside her, then ruffled her hair. "It must have been pretty bad, though, princess," he said sympathetically.

"I've had better days," she admitted, giving him a hug, "but I'll get over it."

"Yes," he agreed. "You have to." He didn't need to say any more. Stephanie knew that he'd seen his best friend killed when they were both in the army in Vietnam. He'd also had to fight for his life. He rarely spoke about it, but the memories were visible on his face some days. Then he smiled. "You ready for dinner?"

Stephanie considered the thought. "Maybe a little," she agreed. Anything to get out of bed!

"Well, it's ready for you," he answered. "And I'm starving." He left the room.

Slipping on her robe, Stephanie joined the others in the kitchen. Her mother had the portable TV on and was watching the news. With a jolt, Stephanie realized that the lead story was David's murder. Mrs. Kirk hastily turned the set off. Dinner was a quiet meal for once. Even Shelly seemed to have cooled down— probably thanks to a warning from her mother. The rest of the evening was just as calm.

Scott called her after dinner. "I'd have come over," he said, concerned. "But your mom said you were resting. How are you feeling?"

"Kind of drained," she admitted, glad to hear his voice.

"Want me to come over?"

She considered the idea. It would mean getting dressed and waiting. Much as she'd like to see him, she wasn't sure she was up to it. "Maybe tomorrow," she suggested. "But thanks for the offer."

"Take care of yourself," he said. "I don't want to have to break in a new girlfriend. I like the one I have right now."

"Flatterer," she said, unable to suppress a smile. "And good night."

After the call Stephanie went to bed again, hoping to sleep but worried that she'd suffer nightmares.

The next thing she knew, it was time to get up, and the day was bright and cheery. It seemed so unreal that she couldn't remember dreaming at all. Later, when she was ready for school and waiting for Nicki, she played with Monty in the yard. The glorious morning seemed so inappropriate. David's family was in mourning. Kimberly's family was struggling with her arrest. And the sun simply ignored all of this pain.

When Nicki arrived, she appeared to be as bright and cheerful as the day. Stephanie was amazed at her friend's resilience. She seemed to be completely unaffected by the previous day's tragedy. Stephanie, on the other hand, couldn't get the images of David out of her mind.

"Well," Nicki commented as she pulled away from the Kirk house, "Blake was really furious last night when you didn't show up. But there wasn't anything he could do. I thought he'd make me do the cleaning, but he caught Paka sniggering and made her do it instead."

"That means he'll be twice as rotten to me tonight, I guess," Stephanie said and sighed. What a prospect to look forward to!

After they reached the school and parked, Stephanie saw a tight cluster of students close by. A large van was parked in the lot, emblazoned with the logo of the local TV station. "What's going on?" she asked.

Nicki rolled her eyes. "Media circus," she explained. "A couple of reporters called us last night. They're all after comments and interviews about the killing."

Stephanie was appalled. She always read a daily newspaper, but it hadn't struck her before that a lot of the information came out only after reporters had intruded into a tragedy. She and Nicki took off for the school as fast as possible.

But not fast enough.

A tall blond woman hurled herself in front of them and extended a microphone with the TV station logo on it. Behind her, a man carrying a huge camcorder across his shoulder managed to wrench himself free of the crowd of students. "And what do you think of the tragic death of your fellow student?" the woman demanded.

"I think you should leave us alone," Stephanie snapped, furious.

Realizing she'd get no quotes from Stephanie, the reporter thrust the mike at Nicki. "And do you have anything to say?"

Nicki gave her a sickly sweet smile. "Yes," she replied and paused for a second to allow the camera to focus on her. "No comment." With another smile, she pushed past the woman.

As they headed for the main entrance, Stephanie glanced back. The reporter, unfazed by rejection, was interviewing other students. Probably those who hadn't even been present. Some of them seemed to be overjoyed at the prospect of appearing on TV. They were probably making up outrageous lies about David and Kimberly. Anger stabbed through her, but what could be done about it? Personal grief had become impersonal news. Freedom of the press and all that.

The media circus made her sick.

# CHAPTER

# 7

~≻

Stephanie heard Scott calling her name and grinned as he joined her and Nicki. He gave her a slow, gentle kiss. "Mmm. You must be feeling better. You *taste* better."

Stephanie laughed. "I'm feeling better *now*," she told him, linking arms with him.

"I'm not," said Nicki, pouting. "Don't I get some of that treatment?"

"Nope," Scott told her. "I'm a one-girl kind of guy."

"Well, I'm one girl," Nicki protested.

"You won't be if you keep flirting with Scott," Stephanie promised her, trying to keep a straight face. It was a good thing she knew Nicki wasn't serious!

Having Scott and Nicki around lightened her mood immensely. She still felt a sharp edge of pain when she thought about David, but Nicki's joking and Scott's concern buoyed her up. Her mind did keep returning to Kimberly, who had nobody she was really close to to fall back on. Stephanie suddenly was struck by the fact that Kimberly didn't have any friends at all. Oh, there were people who hung out with her, but that was all they did. Most of them talked about her behind her back, anyway. Many of them were now saying that they'd always realized Kimberly was on the verge of flaking out, and how terrible she'd been. They were so phony! Stephanie would have despised them if they were worth any deep emotion. As it was, they simply turned her stomach.

Stephanie decided that she'd have to do something nice for Kimberly. She just needed to decide what.

After school she and Nicki drove to the mall. One day's rest from Burger Hell was all she'd get! They made it early, which gave them a chance to clock in before Blake noticed them. When he saw them, though, he scowled ferociously.

"Well, if it isn't the darlings of the media," he grunted. "Are the two of you feeling up to working after yesterday's heroics?"

"Why don't you check the papers and see?" Nicki asked sweetly.

Blake glared at her, then turned to Stephanie. "How about you? Well enough to do a little work today?"

"That's what I'm paid for," she replied, refusing to let him bait her.

"Good. You're on garbage duty. Unless you've got any complaints?"

"No." *It's better than looking at you,* she thought. With a heavy sigh, she settled in, thankful that her shift was just a couple of hours long. She passed her co-worker, but before Paka could say anything, Stephanie said, "I know, I'm a wimp."

"Only sometimes," Paka agreed. "You were pretty cool yesterday, Steph. I wouldn't have touched David. No way!"

"I acted out of desperation, not bravery," Stephanie answered.

"Call it what you like. I wouldn't have done it." Paka flashed her a grin. "And I'm glad you're back. I *hate* garbage duty."

As she cleared out the ruins of the earlier meals, Stephanie recalled her last meeting with Kimberly, when she'd spoken about Dolman. That gave Stephanie an idea.

When work was done, she and Nicki headed back through the crowded mall. It was two hours till closing time. Nicki was distracted by the clothing stores, which gave Stephanie her opening.

"Check some of them out," she suggested. "I want to go down to the antique store."

"That place?" Nicki wrinkled her nose in disgust. "Yuck! What for?"

"Oh, just a thought." Stephanie didn't want to have to explain what it was. "You check out those skirts. I'll meet you here in a few minutes, okay?"

"Okay." Nicki's eyes lit up as she shot into the store.

The antique store was on the lower level of the mall, as was the Burger Heaven, but at the opposite end. The fast-food court was near the entrance, and Dolman's was in the farthest corner from it. When Stephanie reached it, she could see why. It was such a dingy little hole-in-the-wall that the mall managers had probably tried to hide it until they got a chance to push it out entirely. Eyeing what looked like so much old junk, Stephanie pushed open the door and went inside.

The smell hit her first. Musty and ancient, it tickled her nose, making her want to sneeze. She fought back the urge. It took a moment for her eyes to adjust to the dim lighting in the store. The owner seemed to be deliberately making the place appear older than it was. Maybe he thought no one would trust an antique store that looked brand-new? She moved into the store, carefully weaving her way through all kinds of junk—old wicker baskets, wooden boxes and furniture, old bottles and china. It was like walking into an attic, only these things were for sale.

There was nobody else in the place, not even the owner. It felt . . . well, *dead* was probably too strong a word for it, but maybe *sleeping* described it. "Hello?" she called. "Is anyone here?" Maybe he'd gone out for a minute?

Then she heard footsteps in the back room, and Dolman appeared. At least she assumed it was Dolman. Kimberly had said he was a strange old man, but maybe that was just Kimberly being hypercritical as usual. The owner appeared to be in his midfifties. That was old, she supposed, but not *that* old. He had wavy gray hair hanging down over his collar, and piercing blue eyes under shaggy brows. There was a slight stoop to his walk, and he wore a stained and moth-eaten sweater. On his hands were fingerless gloves.

"May I help you?" he asked, stopping behind a small counter. Stephanie had to stop herself from recoiling: his breath smelled as rank as the store.

"I hope so," she said timidly, moving closer, the counter still a barrier between them. Her earlier decision seemed rather foolish when it came to putting it into words. "I'm—um— A friend of mine said she bought a mirror from you recently."

"Did she, now?" His blue eyes bored into hers, and something seemed to stir deep within them. "Her name wouldn't happen to be Kimberly Cullum, would it?"

"That's right." Stephanie nodded eagerly. "You remember her?"

Dolman grunted, then reached under the counter. He tossed a newspaper on the counter, and she saw the headline: "Murder at Local School." Under it was a photo of Kimberly being led off by the police, and below that she saw a couple of smaller pictures. One of them was of Stephanie from the yearbook. Dolman noticed this at the same moment she did and raised one eyebrow.

"According to the paper, you're one of the girls who got her arrested."

"Not exactly," Stephanie replied. "I just tried to help the boy she shot."

Dolman scratched at his nose. Stephanie tried not to shudder at the gross hairs sticking out of his nostrils. Didn't he care about his appearance at all? "Well," he said slowly, "I don't see what this has to do with her buying a mirror from me."

"She said . . ." Stephanie faltered, almost losing her nerve, but then pressed on. "She said the mirror showed her the future. That she saw David kill her in it. That's why she killed him, to stop it from happening."

The store owner laughed. "And you believe that?" He shook his head. "I know teaching standards are down from my days, but I'd have thought they at least made you youngsters understand the difference between real life and fairy stories."

Stung, Stephanie found herself turning red. "I *do* know the difference," she replied. "I didn't say I believed it. I said that's what *she's* claiming."

"I stand corrected," he said mockingly. "Well, I can't help what *she* says, can I?" He tapped the paper with his long fingers. "But *I'd* say that anyone who takes a gun to school and shoots her boyfriend might be expected to say anything. Wouldn't you agree?"

"No," Stephanie replied, surprising herself with the conviction in her voice. "Kimberly isn't that imaginative. I think she really believes what she says. And she *did* buy a mirror from you. You already admitted that."

He studied her shrewdly. "But it's no crime to sell people mirrors. I'm all in favor of gun control, but I really doubt we need mirror control." He chuckled at his own joke. "Then again, maybe we do. Young women these days spend too much time checking mirrors. They're all too conscious of how they look."

*Not you,* Stephanie thought. Aloud, she said, "She came in here with David, the boy who was killed. Did they seem okay to you?"

"I suppose so," he told her, then sighed. "Is there any point to all of these questions? I really am rather busy."

Stephanie couldn't imagine what he could be busy at, since there was no one else in the store. Still, she was taking up his time. "I just wondered if there *might* have been anything—unusual about the mirror that might have set her off."

Dolman snorted. Then he reached up onto a shelf above her head and took down a mirror. "See for yourself," he said. "This is a duplicate of the one she bought."

Stephanie took the mirror. It was intricately and beautifully made, with a twisted candlestick on the handle and a small fairy of some sort grinning at her from the frame. "It's lovely," she said.

"And expensive," he told her. "So be careful with it."

Peering into the perfect glass, she saw herself reflected back. She was a little pale, but that could have been because of the lighting. Carefully, she handed the mirror back to Dolman. "It looks like just a mirror," she admitted.

"It *is* just a mirror," he replied, replacing it on its shelf. "Nothing more, nothing less. It's not magic. It can't show the future."

Stephanie nodded. "I'm sorry I bothered you," she replied. "I guess it was silly of me." She turned to leave.

"Just a minute," Dolman said in a softer voice. She peeked back at him. "You're really worried about your friend, aren't you?"

Nodding, Stephanie said, "I think she's under a terrible strain and that she just snapped. I was just trying to find something—anything—to raise her spirits."

"You're very thoughtful." He twitched his nose. "Look, I feel bad for the girl, too. And . . . well, to be perfectly honest, I had trouble with the police once when I was young." He managed a lopsided smile. "You may not think it, but I was young and wild once, too." He chuckled at a private memory. "I know what it's like in one of those jails. They take away all your own things." He reached under the counter and took out a delicate faux tortoiseshell comb. The top of it was carved into waves, and it was extremely pretty. Stephanie was surprised that he had anything as delightful as this in his shop. "Why don't you take her this? It might cheer her up to be able to do her hair with something lovely."

After placing her bag on the counter, Stephanie

picked up the comb and examined it. It was very beautiful, and she knew he was right—it might be just the thing to cheer Kimberly up, if the police would allow her to have it. "How much does it cost?" she asked, afraid she wouldn't be able to afford it.

Dolman chuckled again. "I'll tell you what," he said. "If I were doing my job properly, it'd be twenty dollars. But for you and your friend—five."

"Okay," she agreed. She suspected he was inflating the price a bit at twenty, but it was definitely worth more than five. "Thanks."

"My pleasure." He watched as she took a bill out of her wallet and passed it over. After she replaced the wallet, she noticed that the comb seemed to ripple in her hand. She gasped as it fell out of her fingers and onto the floor.

"Clumsy," she muttered, picking it up. Surely she'd only imagined that it had tried to get free. As she straightened up, she noticed Dolman moving away from her handbag. Suspiciously, she glanced inside, but her wallet was still there. She was too distrustful of people. She didn't really think he'd been trying to steal her wallet. There wasn't much money left in it, anyway. "Thanks again."

"My pleasure, young lady. I hope your friend has luck." He nodded at the newspaper. "From the sound of things, she's going to need it."

*I guess she will,* thought Stephanie as she left the store. Once outside, she blinked as her eyes became reaccustomed to the glare of the lights. The sound of the crowds of shoppers almost made her flinch. It had been so quiet in Dolman's store!

As she hurried back to Nicki, she couldn't help wondering about the strange man. Something about him made her skin crawl. Maybe it was just that he looked so icky and had such bad breath. In actual fact he had been quite pleasant, and his idea about the comb was a good one. She was uncertain what to make of him.

Nicki was still enjoying herself when Stephanie found her and was reluctant to tear herself away from the skirts she'd been admiring. Stephanie practically had to drag her away from the store and out to her car. As Nicki started the Taurus, Stephanie took the comb from her bag.

"Is there any chance we could stop to see Kimberly on the way home?" she asked.

Nicki glanced at her in surprise. "What for? Don't tell me you're going soft on her?"

"I can't help feeling sorry for her," Stephanie admitted. "She's all alone and friendless in jail."

"She *should* be!" exclaimed Nicki in disgust. "She killed David Blaise, remember?"

"I know that," Stephanie agreed. "And it was horrible. But I *still* can't help feeling sad about her."

"I think you're touched," Nicki muttered. "Oh, hell, why not? They'll probably toss us out. Or maybe I'll get lucky and they'll ask you share a cell with her."

The small jail was in the police station, not far from the high school. Stephanie had never been there

99

before, but she'd passed it many times. A couple of cruisers and a number of other cars were parked outside. Stephanie tried not to stare at the people sitting in the waiting area. They were probably family members of someone who'd been arrested.

A large counter blocked off the far end of the room. A slightly tubby man with a receding hairline was seated behind it, skimming a stack of papers. He looked up as they entered and winked at them.

"Evening, Nicki," he called. "Come to see me or your mom?"

"Hi, Sergeant Estevez," Nicki replied, grinning at him. She nodded at Stephanie. "Actually, my friend here was wondering if she could see Kimberly Cullum for a few minutes. She wants to try to cheer her up. Can you believe it?"

The sergeant scrutinized Stephanie for a minute. "I don't know if she can, but I'll check for you. I don't suppose it would hurt, but the Cullum kid's in on a serious charge." He grimaced. "And her father and that lawyer of his have been burning the captain's ears all day. I think he's still annoyed. Hang on a minute." He vanished through a side door.

"He's a nice guy," Nicki told Stephanie. "He'll do his best because he likes me." She grinned. "Isn't it nice to have connections?"

They had a short wait. Stephanie looked around the waiting area. The other occupants were all locked into their own private spaces. One woman was sobbing softly while a young man dabbed at her eyes with a tissue. Stephanie tried not to stare, glancing at the crime prevention posters and the FBI wanted sheets instead. She felt rather foolish and was afraid that this was a waste of everyone's time.

Then a door opened and the sergeant returned with another police officer. It was a second before Stephanie realized the newcomer was Nicki's mother. She looked so different in her official blues with her hair tucked up under a cap.

"Hi, Mom," Nicki said. "What's the word?"

Mrs. Powers gave a small smile. "The captain agreed to a quick visit," she said. "Though why you want to see Kimberly is beyond me."

"I don't." Nicki shuddered. "I'll stay right here and annoy Sergeant Estevez. It's Steph who feels sorry for Kimberly."

"Okay." Mrs. Powers held the door open. "Come with me, Stephanie."

"Yes, Mrs. Powers—um, ma'am." She didn't know quite what to call her while she was on duty. Normally she saw Nicki's parents when they were civilians! She followed Mrs. Powers through a set of doors, then down two corridors to a small, bleak room. The walls were a dirty shade of cream without any pictures or decorations. Three chairs stood in the middle of the room, each with a small table beside it.

"You'll have to wait here, Stephanie." Mrs. Powers smiled encouragingly. "One of the guards is fetching Kimberly. We'll both have to stay here and watch you, you know."

"Yeah, I sort of guessed that." Stephanie didn't know the procedure; she'd never had to visit anyone in jail before.

"I'll have to hold on to your handbag, too," Mrs. Powers added apologetically. "Regulations."

"In case I'm carrying a gun?" Stephanie joked.

Nicki's mother was quite serious, though. "It's for everyone's protection," she replied. "And I'll have to search you, too. Sorry, but that's a rule as well."

"Okay." Stephanie stood uncomfortably still while Mrs. Powers gently but expertly patted her down.

"You're clean," she announced, then grinned. "Not that I really thought you had an assault rifle under your skirt." She reached for Stephanie's handbag.

Before she handed it over, Stephanie took the comb out. "Would it be okay for me to give Kimberly this?" she asked, showing it to Mrs. Powers. "I thought it would cheer her up."

Nicki's mother frowned and examined the comb. "It's very pretty," she commented. She played with the tines for a moment, seeing them bend. "I guess it'll be okay. Metal combs are forbidden, but this is soft plastic."

Stephanie remembered what Nicki had said about the suicide watch. They were obviously being very careful. Clutching the comb in both hands, Stephanie waited. A moment later the barred door at the far end of the room opened. A tall, muscular woman with an impassive face led Kimberly into the room. Stephanie gasped at how terrible Kimberly looked.

She was dressed in very loose pajama-style clothing

and wore slippers that slapped the floor as she walked. Her long black hair was obviously unwashed and tangled. She wore no makeup, and her eyes were puffed and red-rimmed, probably from crying. Her right hand was bandaged. The guard led her to the middle chair and gently pushed her into the seat. Then she retreated to the door.

Stephanie slipped into the seat facing her. "Hi, Kimberly," she said softly. "How are you feeling?"

"Dreadful." Kimberly's eyes were as dull as her hair. "Have you come to make fun of me? Glad to see me here?"

"No!" Stephanie was hurt by the accusation. "I thought you might just like someone to talk to. It must be dreadful here."

The other girl was surprised. "You really mean that?" she asked.

"Of course." Stephanie held out the comb. "I brought this for you. I thought you might like something pretty."

Kimberly stared at the comb, then clutched it in her left hand. She managed a feeble smile. "Thanks, Stephanie. I really appreciate it." She used her bandaged hand to push some of her hair away from her face. "My hair's a mess, isn't it?"

"Sort of," Stephanie agreed. She really didn't know what to say. "Um . . . are you going to be getting out of here on bail or something?"

Kimberly shook her head. "They've denied me bail," she said quietly. "I'm really pissing off my father's lawyer by wanting to plead guilty, too. I'm probably going to do him out of a million dollars in legal fees." She tried to smile at her joke, but Stephanie could see the tears at the corners of her eyes. "Maybe you'd better go now. I'm not in the best shape, you know."

Nodding, Stephanie stood up. "I'll come back to see you," she promised. "If you want me to, that is."

Kimberly nodded as she rose. "Yeah. That'd be nice." She seemed embarrassed. "I don't know why you're doing this. I've always been rotten to you. Be honest, now, haven't I?"

"Yeah," Stephanie agreed. "But right now I think you need a friend more than you need another enemy, don't you?"

"Do I ever." Kimberly brushed at her eyes, then her nose, with the back of her hand. "Thanks, Stephanie. I really appreciate this." The guard came toward her, and she wandered away, clutching the comb in her hand.

Stephanie managed to give her a smile before the barred door separated them. She turned back to find Mrs. Powers waiting for her, holding out her bag. Stephanie took it back. "She seems depressed."

"Yes, she does," Nicki's mother agreed. "But jail isn't supposed to be amusing. After all, she *killed* a boy."

"I know that." Stephanie shook her head. "But I can't help feeling sorry for her." As Mrs. Powers led the way back, Stephanie asked, "What's likely to happen to her?"

"That will depend on what happens in court," Mrs.

Powers replied. "Since her father can buy as many experts as he needs, I suspect she'll get away with an insanity plea. Then she'll be hospitalized until she's better. *If* she gets better." She grimaced. "Personally, I think she'd be better off just pleading guilty and doing jail time. At least she could be certain of getting out of a cell."

Stephanie shuddered at the thought of spending the rest of one's life in a mental hospital.

# CHAPTER
8

"Well, I hope you feel better now," Nicki grumbled as they left the police station. "I was going to wash my hair tonight, but it's too late now."

Glancing at her watch, Stephanie saw it was after nine. "I'm sorry, Nicki. And I wouldn't say *better* is how I feel. Worse, if anything. Kimberly is so miserable."

Nicki shook her head. *"Kimberly* is so miserable?" she echoed incredulously. "Listen, Steph, I just don't get you right now. *She's* the one who killed David, remember. She *deserves* to be miserable. She isn't the victim here."

Stephanie realized that Nicki was being serious for

once. "I don't understand me, either," she admitted. "But . . . well, I think Kimberly *is* a victim somehow. I just haven't figured out how yet."

"I think your brains are fried," Nicki replied bluntly as she unlocked her car.

"Maybe they are," Stephanie agreed with a sigh. She slid into the passenger seat beside Nicki. "I just don't know. I feel so torn and so confused."

Nicki started the car, then grinned. "Ah, I bet you're still suffering from shock. You're not as resilient as I am."

"Maybe it is shock." Stephanie didn't know. She had been feeling all the strain piling up on her— pressures at school, at work, at home—and then the shooting. It seemed sometimes that the world was piling as much as it could onto her shoulders until she broke under the load. Maybe Kimberly had felt something like that and just snapped . . .

Or maybe she was telling the truth: maybe there *had* been something odd about the mirror she'd bought. There was certainly something odd about Dolman. It wasn't any one thing she could point to, but she was quite certain that he was somehow . . . well, *wrong*.

She gave up trying to figure it out. Instead, she started to dig in her bag for a tissue. She found two empty packs that she hadn't thrown out before she found one with a couple left in it. Blowing her nose made her feel a little better. She really had to clean out her bag. It was getting harder and harder to find things. Plus she was carrying around so much excess weight she'd lose five pounds instantly.

Nicki dropped her off and waved good night. Stephanie waved back, then dug in the bag for her keys. The ring came out tangled with a hair clip, and she had to struggle with it to free the door key. That was *definitely* enough! It was way beyond time to clean out the junk. Inside, her father was watching some cop show on TV. She gave him a quick kiss and waved to her mother, who was working on yet another batch of papers at the kitchen table. She dumped her bag on her bed, then headed back to the kitchen to pour herself a glass of soda.

"How's it going?" she asked her mother, gesturing toward the stack of papers.

"Pretty well," Mrs. Kirk replied. "Things are really clicking at work. I'm starting to feel wanted again."

"You're *always* wanted," Stephanie replied.

"So are you," her mother said with a smile. "But not right now. It's hard enough to concentrate with that rubbish your father's watching going. I don't need more distractions."

"I can take a hint." Stephanie wandered down the hall to her room. She saw a bar of light under Shelly's door but heard no noise. Her sister was probably listening to music with her earphones on. That was a relief. Shelly had terrible taste in music. Stephanie closed her door to keep out the sound of screeching brakes and overloud commercials from the TV, and then sat on her bed. She upended her handbag and started to sort through the junk.

Out went the dead tissue packs. There was a receipt for something she couldn't recall buying from one of the stores in the mall. That went into the wastebasket as well. So did a handful of rubber bands and paper clips. She dropped her wallet back into the bag along with her lipstick. There was an old one as well, and that got tossed. The hair clips she threw onto her dresser.

Then she paused.

On her comforter, clearly visible now that most of the junk was gone, was a brooch she had never seen before. Puzzled, she picked it up. It was about three inches long and an inch and a half wide. It appeared to be made of silver and was in the shape of a scarab beetle. Its eyes were inlaid gems—maybe fake, but they seemed awfully real. It had six little silver legs, and on the underside was a long straight pin.

Stephanie carefully examined the fine, detailed workmanship of the brooch. If it was actually silver and those were real gems, not cubic zirconiums, then it had to be worth a small fortune. Maybe even a pretty decent-size fortune. Where had the brooch come from? How had it gotten into her bag? It looked like an—

The truth hit her suddenly, and she drew in a sharp breath.

It was quite clearly an antique. And there was only one place it could have come from—Dolman's store. She had suspected him of taking something *out* of her bag, but instead, he'd put something *into* it. This valuable brooch.

But why?

She didn't think for even a second it was because he liked her. He was pretty repulsive, but he hadn't been trying to come on to her. So this wasn't a gift. Then what was it?

If it wasn't a gift and she hadn't taken it, then only one possibility came to mind. He had placed it in her bag so that he could accuse her of having stolen it. He was trying to make her look like a thief! But why would he do that?

The only reason she could come up with was that she'd been checking out Kimberly's story. Was Dolman afraid she'd talk the police into doing that, too? Was this his way of making her look like a trouble-maker and thief so that if she accused him of anything, she wouldn't be believed? Her idea was sounding farfetched now, though. She hadn't actually accused Dolman of anything except maybe knowing more about the mirror he'd sold to Kimberly than he was letting on. There was no crime in that. So why would he worry about her talking to the police? As if they'd believe her!

Besides which she couldn't bring herself to believe that there was truth to this magic mirror nonsense. Only that Kimberly *believed* there was. She wasn't ruling out the possibility that Kimberly had cracked under pressure. She could only guess at the sort of strain the other girl might be under.

Stephanie stared at the brooch, completely at a loss.

If Dolman was trying to frame her for theft, he must be worried that she knew something tying him to David's murder.

Which could only mean there *was* some link between the disgusting old man and the shooting. And there was only one connecting link—the mirror. Kimberly claimed it had influenced the murder, and Dolman's actions seemed to confirm that claim.

Still, the brooch hadn't exactly been hidden in her bag. Maybe he'd intended her to find it as a warning: *Talk to the police, and I can get you into trouble.* Well, she could settle that quite simply. All she had to do was return the brooch on her way to work the next day. She could slip it back into the shop without his spotting her, she was sure of that. Then he'd have no hold over her at all.

She felt a wave of exhaustion. It had been a long and very tiring day. There would be plenty of time in the morning to think about all this again. For the moment she placed the brooch on her dressing table. Then, on second thought, she put it back into her handbag. Shelly had a habit of poking around, and she didn't want her kid sister asking any awkward questions. Then she finished repacking her bag. Satisfied, she yawned and stretched. Time to get ready for bed.

"Time for bed," the guard called.

Kimberly blinked her eyes, wrenching herself back to reality with a shudder. Reality at the moment was far and away too depressing to stay connected to for long. The tiny cell was closing in around her—the bare, dirty walls, the small, hard bed and single sheet, the tiny barred window high on the wall, the sink, and the toilet. That was it. There was nowhere to go, and no privacy, even to use the toilet. She knew she was on a suicide watch; every fifteen minutes the guard checked out the cell to make sure she hadn't either escaped or killed herself.

The idea was almost tempting. Kimberly was depressed enough to think that killing herself had to be a step up from this situation. Only a few days earlier she'd been in her own large, comfortable room with a walk-in closet filled with as many clothes as she wanted. Now she was sitting on a hard bed in a small cell, wearing prison rags. All she was allowed was a loose-fitting pajama suit—a top that slipped on (no buttons or zippers—she might kill herself by choking on them) and loose trousers (no elastic—she might use it to make a noose and hang herself). She wasn't even allowed a bra for the same reason. She had slippers with no laces or anything that could be used for a suicide. Instead of selecting from her extensive wardrobe, she now only picked out a clean pair of panties once a day.

She felt utterly degraded. No perfumes, not even her Aqua Keri. Just a plain bar of soap—barely more than a sliver. A little shampoo for the shower she was allowed from time to time. No makeup or nail polish. Not even a pair of tweezers—she might slash her wrists with them somehow. No mirror, so she couldn't see how dragged out and disgusting she looked—she might break it and use the glass to kill herself.

Kimberly had to admit that the police were really inventive when it came to thinking up ways she might commit suicide. She half suspected that they wouldn't give her cereal for fear that she might stick her face into the bowl and drown herself in the milk.

Time for bed—big deal. What was there to do? She couldn't get a warm drink and settle down with a nice book. Or watch a little late-night TV. She pulled back the single sheet and slid under it. Lying on her back, she stared up at the ceiling. The light in the cell would be turned out in a couple of minutes, but the one in the corridor outside the bars would stay on all night. The guard had to be able to see her when she came round to check.

And every fifteen minutes the guard would walk down the corridor and peer into the cell, just in case . . . It was so humiliating to be checked up on like that. She'd learned to use the toilet *after* the guard made her rounds.

Kimberly let her mind drift. It was easy to do that, she'd discovered. Just to stop paying attention, to float away. There was little else for her to do. Eat, do a few exercises, and then just wait to go to bed each day. Her father and his lawyer had visited exactly twice. Her mother hadn't come at all. Both her parents were bitterly ashamed of her and angry with her. The lawyer—she couldn't even remember his name—was simply frustrated. He was arranging for a psychological evaluation. She wasn't sure that he believed she was crazy, but he seemed to think that everyone else would.

Maybe he was right. Maybe she was crazy. She'd been so freaked out by that mirror that maybe there was no hope of her ever being normal again. Killing David had seemed to be the only way out. Now she envied him. He'd been driven just as crazy. In that last second as she'd shot him again and again, she'd seen his eyes. There was no hatred in them—just a profound relief that he'd moved beyond the horror that was haunting him. She'd realized then that he must have seen his own fate in that mirror, too.

If she hadn't been so stunned, she might have thought to turn the gun on herself and blow out her brains. It was the last chance she'd had to escape. She'd lost it now. Then Nicki Powers had jumped her and broken her hand.

It still hurt, even with the medication. She didn't particularly care, actually. After all, she wasn't using the hand for anything much, was she?

She tried to think about David, to feel sorry for him or to feel remorse for what she had done. She knew she ought to feel sorrow and shame, but she simply didn't. The only emotions she felt were for herself—boredom, mostly, and embarrassment. And a sense that she was still being haunted somehow, even though that mirror had been destroyed.

The only good thing that had happened to her was that visit from Stephanie Kirk, and her gift of the comb. Kimberly couldn't understand Stephanie's motives. Why had she been so kind to her? Kimberly had never done anything nice to *her*. On the contrary. Yet the only person who'd shown her any compassion at all was the one she'd least expected it from. It didn't make any sense.

Then again, nothing much made sense now.

There was the sound of footsteps, which stopped outside her cell. *I'm still here,* she thought. *And still alive, worst luck.* The footsteps started up again, retreating. They'd be back in fifteen minutes. What an exciting event to look forward to!

Then she became vaguely aware of another sound. A kind of dry, scratching noise. Puzzled, she concentrated on listening. The scritchy sound was faint, but definitely there. It sounded like a mouse or some other small animal moving, she thought. But there were no mice in the building. She would almost have welcomed the company if there were.

She rolled onto her side and peered across the cell. Because of the light in the corridor, the small room was clearly visible. The scrabbling sound was coming from the sink. Maybe some animal had climbed up the drain? She knew spiders did that, but this was too loud to be a spider. She was tempted to get out of bed and take a look, but she knew that was against the rules. Instead, she lay still, barely breathing, waiting to discover whether whatever was making that sound would move into view.

Kimberly realized at that moment how far she'd sunk. A few days ago she could have done anything she liked. She could have driven off in her BMW or played music or watched TV. She could have gone shopping or invited people over. And here she was, in this cold, uncomfortable bed, waiting to see if a mouse would peer over the edge of her sink. And this was the high point of her day. . . .

There was a shiver of movement, and something appeared on the rim of the sink. It took her several seconds to realize what it was, and even then she couldn't believe it.

It looked like a huge insect, several inches long. Dozens of tiny legs trembled and moved slowly. What looked like feelers seemed to bend and sway in the still air. But it wasn't an insect at all.

It was the comb that Stephanie had brought her.

She'd placed it on the sink after she combed out her hair. Now, somehow, it was moving, using its tines as legs to scuttle about on.

This was totally crazy! Combs couldn't come to life! They didn't clamber upright and start to walk. This was just too absurd!

This one didn't seem to know that. It paused for a few heartbeats, looking for all the world as if it were thinking. Then, in a flash, it jumped down to the floor. She stared at it in shock as it stood on its gently swaying tines and seemed to sniff the air. Kimberly wanted to laugh, the whole thing was so unbelievable. But it was also scary. The comb was acting as if it were alive, not some inanimate object.

Maybe she really *had* gone insane. This couldn't possibly be happening. She stared at the comb and had the terrifying impression that it was aware of her and that it was staring back, watching her somehow. There appeared to be some kind of malevolent life to the tiny thing.

It scuttled across the floor toward the bed.

Kimberly wanted to scream, to shout out in terror, but she wasn't able to make a sound. She shuddered uncontrollably, trying to crawl away from the edge of the bed. The comb stopped, faced her, and seemed to gather itself together.

Then it sprang up from the floor, leaping for the bed.

Kimberly jumped back, slamming into the wall, as the comb paused on the edge of the cover, its tines moving like insect feet. It took a couple of small steps toward her. She whimpered, pure fear coursing through her ice-cold body as she stared at the comb.

She managed one thin, shrill scream as the comb leaped at her throat. . . .

The guard snapped to attention when she heard the scream. It was probably just the Cullum girl having a bad dream. A spoiled brat, that one, and definitely touched in the head. But she couldn't take a chance. Jumping to her feet, she ran to the cell door and stared inside.

Then she shuddered at what she saw.

The stench of blood made her want to gag. Kimberly lay sprawled out on the bed, her head lolling over the edge, her dark hair a cascade to the floor. Her long throat was exposed, and the guard could see the long, jagged, raw wound ripped across it.

# CHAPTER

# 9

Stephanie woke from a nightmare, writhing and whimpering softly. She'd been dreaming of being attacked by insects, with hundreds of horrible, chitinous bodies and thousands of tiny legs crawling all over her. Gasping, she blinked and realized with relief that it was morning, almost time to get up, and that there were no bugs in bed with her. There was a film of perspiration on her skin, though, and she felt uncomfortable, almost stifled. Her nightie was sticking to her skin. She couldn't remember all the details of her nightmare—thank goodness!— but it must really have spooked her. The image of the insects had been all too real, and she shuddered.

As soon as she heard her father get up and head into the kitchen to start the coffee, she jumped out of bed and claimed the bathroom before Shelly. She clipped up her hair and took a shower, washing away the stickiness of the night. That made her feel much better. Wrapped in her robe, she opened the bathroom door and stood aside as Shelly charged in. Then she headed for the kitchen and poured herself a cup of coffee. Her father gave her a smile over the top of his paper, then buried himself again in the pages. Sipping at the coffee, Stephanie returned to her room.

She opened the blinds just enough to see out. It was going to be a wonderful early spring day—the sky was clear. Opening her closet, she picked out her flowered culottes and a white blouse. Perhaps today all her grim thoughts might dissipate. It would be lovely just to be able to relax again. As she prepared for school, though, she remembered the scarab brooch and the cheeriness of the day diminished.

Was that why she'd dreamed about insects?

She tried to recover her earlier mood, but it had vanished. Dread rolled inside her, like a cold, hard rock in her stomach. Something told her that this was going to be a truly dreadful day. She shook her head to convince herself that her premonition was silly, but the certainty refused to leave.

She was thankful that today was Friday—and not the thirteenth, either! She didn't have to work on Fridays, and she'd at least be out of school for a couple of days, even though she had to work on Saturday. Maybe she and Scott could get together and have a little fun. She needed to do something to take her mind off everything. Or did Scott have baseball practice on Sunday? Between her job and his practices, they were spending less and less time together.

Stephanie was still feeling a little blue when Nicki arrived to pick her up for school. For once, though, Nicki was in a worse mood than Stephanie, and she was only too eager to explain why.

"Kimberly's dead," she announced as she pulled away from the Kirk house.

The dull, hard stone in Stephanie sank another few inches, gained several pounds, and turned ice-cold. "Dead?" she repeated numbly. "But—how?"

"Mom got a call this morning," Nicki replied, evading the question. "It happened around eleven last night apparently."

*"What* happened?" asked Stephanie. She wasn't sure she really wanted to hear the answer, but she had to know. "How did she die?"

Nicki gave her a very odd look, then yelped and concentrated on driving as she narrowly missed plowing into the oncoming traffic. "She killed herself."

"Oh, God." Stephanie shuddered. "Horrible!" Then a thought struck her. "How could she do that? I thought you said she was on a suicide watch?"

"She was." Nicki risked another look, as if sizing up Stephanie's mood. "But she managed to slit her own throat, anyway."

The image in Stephanie's mind was terrible, and she shivered. "With what?" she finally asked. "I thought they took everything away from her."

"They did." Nicki could hold out no longer. "The only thing she could have used was the comb you gave her last night."

Stephanie felt as if a bomb had gone off inside her head. There was a sharp pain between her eyes and a bile taste in her mouth. "It was my fault?" she asked almost in a whisper. The pain was physical now and intense.

"That's what they think," Nicki admitted. She acted very guilty for having to hurt her friend. "Don't blame yourself, Steph. You couldn't have known she'd do it."

"But it was a *plastic* comb," Stephanie protested, trying to deny the guilt that was gnawing at the edges of her mind. "She couldn't have—"

"Yeah, it sounds pretty wild to me, too," agreed Nicki. "I mean, *my* comb wouldn't even cut butter, let alone my jugular." Seeing Stephanie go pale, she said, "Oops. Excuse my stupid remark. Anyway, there's something really strange about this."

*"Everything's* strange about this," said Stephanie weakly. *It's my fault,* she thought. *I killed Kimberly.*

"Yeah, but I mean mega-strange," replied Nicki. "They couldn't find the comb afterward."

"What?" Stephanie shook her head. "Wasn't it in her hand?"

"No. In fact, it wasn't even in her *cell."* Nicki's

expression was grim. "That sounds really bizarre to me. I mean, if she managed to cut open a vein with the comb, she had to have been clutching it hard. But the guard said she heard a scream, and when she reached the cell, Kimberly was dead and her hands were empty. They searched the cell several times, and the comb had *vanished.*"

It was hard for Stephanie to follow all this. "But where could it have gone?"

"God knows—and apparently nobody else. The captain's having a cow about the whole thing. He's afraid the police are going to look really stupid once the reporters start feasting on this."

"It's all my fault," said Stephanie, almost moaning. She hadn't realized how bad she could feel before this. "I just wanted to help, and I killed her."

"No, you didn't!" snapped Nicki. Abruptly she pulled the car over to the side of the road and slammed on the brakes. Then she glared at Stephanie. "The most you did was to provide Kimberly with the opportunity. It was *her* decision to kill herself, not yours. So stop feeling guilty about it."

"That's easy for you to say," Stephanie muttered. She could feel tears welling up in her eyes, and snatched a tissue out of her bag to dab at them.

"Well, I'd say the most you can blame yourself for is stupidity," Nicki told her roughly. "How did you come up with such a dumb idea—buying her a comb?"

This penetrated Stephanie's guilt and pain. It was

as if a light had gone on in the dim recesses of her mind. "I didn't," she whispered. "It was Dolman's idea."

"Dolman?"

"Yes." Stephanie blew her nose and tried to pull herself together. *"He* suggested that I take her the comb." She shifted in the seat. "Do you think he could have known she might use it to kill herself?"

"I don't see how," Nicki answered, puzzled. "Besides, why would he want her dead?"

"I don't know," Stephanie admitted. "But she *was* telling people that she killed David because of a mirror she bought from Dolman. Now she's dead because of a comb I bought for her from Dolman."

Nicki's face creased in a frown. "That's a bit wild, isn't it?"

"Yes," agreed Stephanie. "And it gets wilder." She opened her purse and removed the scarab brooch. "I found this in my handbag when I got home last night. Dolman must have slipped it in."

Nicki took the brooch and examined it. "Jeez, this must be worth a fortune!" She glanced at Stephanie, then back at the brooch. "You think he likes you?"

"God, I hope not." The thought was repulsive. "I saw him near my handbag and thought he was trying to steal my wallet. Instead, he was planting that."

"Planting?" Nicki caught on fast. "You think he means to report it stolen?"

"I can't think why else he'd do it." Stephanie took the brooch and replaced it in her bag. "Kimberly won't be accusing him of anything, and I think that brooch is his insurance that I won't."

Nicki sat quietly for a moment staring into space, her hands on the steering wheel. Stephanie saw how white her knuckles were. She had to be really gripping the wheel—a link to reality? Finally Nicki sighed. "I wish I could say that this is so much doggie doo, but I know you better than that, Steph. You're weird, but even you're not *this* weird."

"Gee, thanks. What a friend you are." Stephanie felt hope rising within her. "So . . . what do you think?"

"Something very odd is going on here." Nicki chewed her lower lip for a moment, then faced Stephanie. "There is a link somehow with this Dolman character. Okay, he got you to take the comb to Kimberly, then set up an excuse to accuse you of theft, or at least threaten to accuse you. And if he did have something to do with David's death, I can imagine he'd want to shut Kimberly up. But how could he possibly have been certain she'd use the comb to kill herself?" She sighed out loud. "The surgeon general ought to stick a warning label on you: 'Stephanie Kirk can be dangerous or fatal to your mental health.'"

"I'm starting to think that myself," agreed Stephanie. "But he's got to be up to something."

"I'm sure he is." Nicki eased the car back onto the road again. "Look, hang on to that brooch," she suggested. "Keep it safe—*very* safe! I'll call my dad from work after school. He and mom can keep an ear open for a report from Dolman about a theft. You should be safe on that score. Maybe I can talk one of them into taking the brooch back before he can report it stolen. He wouldn't dare complain then. And I'll suggest they do a background check on the guy. I wonder where he had his store before the mall opened?"

"I don't care," said Stephanie firmly. "I'd be happy if they could somehow just brick him up inside it."

"That might be a bit extreme," Nicki replied, grinning. "Hey, I'm starting to enjoy this. I feel like a real detective already."

Stephanie wished she had her friend's cheerful nature. "I'd feel more like enjoying it if two people weren't already dead," she replied. "But I admit that I'm feeling less guilty about the whole business now."

Her mood improved another few notches when they reached the school. As they were heading inside, Scott joined them. He was in a boisterous mood, grabbing Stephanie and kissing her. "Hiya, gorgeous."

"Hiya, hunk," she replied a little breathlessly. "What's gotten into you today?"

"Spring," he said, kissing the tip of her nose. "A young man's fancy turns, and all that."

"My stomach turns," muttered Nicki.

"Plus, practice after school today has been canceled," Scott added. "You want to check out a movie tonight? I'll even let you pick which one."

"I'd love to," Stephanie said. "I really could do with a break."

"Okay." He lifted her chin and gave her another kiss. "I'll pick you up at six. Surprise me with what we'll see." He hurried off to his first class.

Feeling better, Stephanie watched him go. Nicki rolled her eyes in mock disgust.

"It's repulsive," she commented. "You're putty in his hands."

"You're just jealous," Stephanie retorted.

"True," Nicki agreed cheerfully.

"Well, why don't you find yourself a guy and join us?" suggested Stephanie. "It's been *ages* since we doubled."

"I'd love to," Nicki replied. "But it's not easy finding the right guy, you know. I'm so stunningly beautiful, witty, and sexy that I scare most boys off. I think you got the last good guy in town."

"What about Mike Yarr?" suggested Stephanie.

"Mike Yarr?" Nicki repeated incredulously. "Mr. Macho? Give me a break! I'd sooner date Henry Blake." She pulled a face. "And you can't get lower than that."

Stephanie laughed. She felt so much better now. She'd felt so dreadful at first, thinking she might have been responsible for Kimberly's suicide. Now she was sure that Dolman had somehow planned the whole thing. Nicki was finally starting to listen to her suspicions, and maybe her parents could get a line on that creepy old guy. That night she'd have fun with Scott. The day was definitely better.

As long as she kept avoiding thoughts about Kimberly. That was the only dark cloud in her bright sky right then.

Scott was just about to leave the otherwise empty men's room when the door slammed open. Brent Wardlow and his two single-digit-IQ friends slouched in, mean grins on their faces. Brent pretended to be surprised, but Scott realized that the thug had been planning this meeting.

"Well," Brent said. "Look who we've bumped into, guys."

"Yeah," commented the taller of his stooges. "Didn't that used to be Scott Berman?"

Scott let his backpack fall to the floor. They were between him and the door this time, and they obviously did not intend to let him pass. Three against one—those weren't good odds, especially when the three of them obviously meant to inflict serious damage to the one of him. Scott could feel his adrenaline surging, but he knew he was likely to get creamed if he couldn't talk them out of fighting. To the best of his knowledge, nobody had ever talked Brent out of anything. He sighed theatrically. "Knock it off," he suggested, trying to inject more confidence and attitude into his voice than he really possessed. His act didn't fool them for a second.

"I told you we'd get even," Brent said softly. "Nobody disses me and gets away with it, Berman. Nobody."

Scott kept his eyes on Brent, but was aware that the two others were moving on either side of him. There was no way this would be a fair fight. That wasn't Brent's style. He preferred the bulldozer approach— leave your victims looking as if a bulldozer had run over them. It went against the grain for Scott to fight, but if he didn't, he was going to end up with serious medical bills. "Tell you what," he said, just as softly. "I'll give you the respect you deserve. Just as soon as you deserve any." He lashed out and kicked the garbage can beside the sink toward the thug on the left.

The kid yelped as it slammed painfully into his shins. The other stooge jumped for him, but Scott wasn't standing still for the attack. He knew that Brent would wait for his companions to grab and hold Scott before he dirtied his hands, which meant taking out the two of them was a priority. Twisting to one side, Scott grabbed his attacker's right hand and jerked him forward as he swung around. The boy's stomach and one of the sinks connected very loudly.

Brent was taken aback by this turn of events, but he hadn't made a reputation as a bully for nothing. Though he'd wanted his assistants to grab Scott, he wasn't a total coward. With a growl, he jumped for Scott, his fist swinging. Scott tried to move, but he couldn't disentangle himself fast enough. Brent's blow caught him across the side of the neck, sending a stab of pain down through his shoulder. But it also brought Brent within reach and blocked off the first thug.

Scott spun around, trying to ignore the pain in his shoulder, and punched Brent in the stomach. His leather jacket absorbed most of the blow, though. He grunted and flinched, but the punch hadn't done him any real damage. He hammered his fist into Scott's side, sending another wave of agony through Scott. Scott managed to bring his hand around for a stinging smack across Brent's face, but then he was grabbed from behind by Brent's friend. Before he could get free, Brent punched him again, harder, in the stomach.

All the breath exploded from Scott's lungs, and pain made everything go black for a second. He tried to get his feet into motion. If he could kick backward, maybe he could pull free. He never got the chance. Brent grabbed a handful of Scott's hair and jerked his head forward, bringing his other elbow up at the same moment. Agony flashed across Scott's face, and he could smell blood in his nostrils.

Then the door to the corridor opened. "Wardlow!"

Through a haze, Scott saw that the gym teacher, Mr. Cavelli, was standing in the doorway, a furious expression on his face. Brent paused, his fist drawn back ready for another punch at Scott, aware he'd been caught literally red-handed, with blood from Scott's nose on his hand. Seizing his chance, Scott shook himself free from the loosened grip of his captor.

All three of the bullies stared at Mr. Cavelli, guilt

and irritation written all over their faces. The gym teacher glowered at them. "Outside," he ordered. "Now!" Brent paused, and his two thugs looked at him uncertainly, waiting for his instructions. "Now!" barked Mr. Cavelli. Brent slouched forward, his two shadows in his wake.

The teacher turned to Scott. "You okay?"

"Oh, just fine," Scott muttered. His face and side hurt like the blazes, and he could feel the blood from his nose trickling down his face.

"You'd better see the nurse," Mr. Cavelli ordered. "Wardlow and his cronies have an appointment with the principal." He stomped out after the trio, letting the door swing shut.

*Terrific,* thought Scott, turning painfully to the sink. He managed to splash water on his face, then dabbed at the mess with a paper towel. Somehow he doubted that a few words from the principal and detention would really influence Brent all that much. Which meant that Scott had escaped for the moment, but he was going to have to keep a wary eye open from now on. And stick with his friends a little more. He studied his face in the mirror. His nose was swollen a little, but that was about it. The pain in his side was subsiding, too. He stood up and winced. He'd better see the nurse, anyway. Mr. Cavelli would undoubtedly check on him.

It had started out as a pretty good day, too.

# CHAPTER

# 10

Stephanie smiled at Scott as he stopped his car outside the Kirk house. She'd had a good evening and had enjoyed the film. He'd winced a bit when she clung to his arm during the action scenes, but she—like the rest of the class—had heard about his run-in earlier that day with Brent. It hurt her to think of what Scott had gone through, but Brent and his friends were being punished for it. There was nothing she could do, except comfort Scott.

"That was fun," she told him. "Thank you." Leaning forward, she kissed him gently on the lips. He responded very nicely and then slipped an arm around her shoulders to hold her close. She pulled back a few inches, looking at him. "Are you feeling better now?" she asked.

"Mmm . . . I'm not sure," he said. "Try again and we'll see."

She kissed him again, longer this time. It was harder to pull back after that, mostly because she wasn't completely sure she wanted to. "Well?" she asked.

"Better," he replied, "but not completely well." This time he leaned forward to kiss her. She slipped her arm around him and enjoyed the experience. She wasn't entirely certain what her feelings for him were, but there was absolutely no denying that he was a great kisser. All her stress was washed away in the enjoyment she felt.

Then she felt his hand on her knee, stroking gently. A moment later it started to inch upward. Stephanie pulled back from the kiss and gave him a mock frown. "That hand better stop right where it is," she told him gently. It froze in place, and she could see the disappointment in his eyes. "You know how I feel about it," she reminded him. When they first started dating, she had told him how she felt. He could accept it, or find another girl. He'd accepted—then.

"I was kind of hoping things had changed between us a little," he told her.

"They have—a little." Stephanie kissed his nose. "I'm very fond of you, Scott. But I'm not sure it's more than that yet. Can you understand?"

"I guess."

"You're mad at me," she said quietly.

"No," he said, perhaps a little too quickly. "Well," he amended, "not mad. Frustrated, maybe. I mean, we've been going steady for six months now—"

"And all you get is a good-night kiss," finished Stephanie. "Scott, when we started dating I told you I don't believe I have to pay for dates with sex. My beliefs haven't changed, and they *won't* change." She gave him a smile. "If you can't accept that, then maybe we'd better stop dating. I know you could find a dozen other girls."

"But I don't want another girl," he complained. "I want *you.*" His face twisted as he grimaced. "Obviously in ways you don't want me."

"I didn't say that," she replied honestly. "I've got hormones, too, you know. But I'm not going to let them control me—or ruin my life."

"You think I'd ruin your life?" he asked her, hurt.

"Not purposely," she answered. "I've been thinking quite the opposite, in fact. But I'm not going to risk our relationship and our future together. I don't think that's good." She gazed into his eyes. "Do you?"

He sighed. "No, not really. But there are times when I'd like to chance it."

"Chances you can take in sports," she replied. "Not with my life, and not with yours." She kissed him again and then got out of the car. "Good night, Scott."

"'Night."

Stephanie watched the car pull away, biting her lip. She knew that Scott didn't really *want* to understand her feelings on the issue. But she also knew that he really did and that he respected her beliefs. Still, she wished he knew how hard it was for her sometimes to stick to those beliefs herself!

She let herself into the house. Monty was asleep behind the front door. He managed to open one eye to check on the "intruder" and then closed it again when he recognized her. "What a greeting," she muttered.

Her parents were cuddled up on the couch, watching some old black-and-white movie on TV. Her father winked at her. "Hi, princess. Have a good time?"

"Mmmm," she agreed. "It was fun." She glanced at the screen. It was a Humphrey Bogart movie. "I guess I'll get ready for bed now. G'night." They were back watching the movie before she was out of the room.

The bathroom door was closed as she passed it. It had to be Shelly getting ready for bed. Entering her room, Stephanie dropped her bag onto the chair, then kicked off her shoes. It felt good to be out of them. While she was waiting for Shelly to finish, Stephanie changed into her nightie and slipped on her robe. As she brushed out her hair, she couldn't help thinking about Scott.

She knew he had been honest with her, and she appreciated that. She just wished he could understand her point of view. Still, it had to be hard for him. Some of the guys he hung out with loved to brag about their conquests, real or imaginary. Scott had to feel like the odd man out, and that couldn't be easy on him. On the other hand, she had absolutely no intention of giving in to his pressures just because she felt sorry for him. He'd have to learn to cope—or get a new girlfriend.

The idea that he might drop her *did* hurt. She wasn't sure if she was really in love with him, but she was very fond of him. Scott was a great person to be around, and he made her feel good. It wouldn't be easy to let him go. In fact, it was never easy to tell him to stop, either. Stephanie knew that to Scott she sounded very firm and sure of herself. She also knew that making herself tell him to stop often took a great deal of willpower.

"It's all yours," Shelly yelled through her door.

Stephanie jumped. She'd been so lost in her thoughts she'd forgotten about her sister. As she left her room, Stephanie almost ran into Shelly, who was hovering outside her door.

"You and Scott have the most boring romance *ever,*" she complained.

Stephanie glared at her sister. "Were you spying on us?" she demanded.

"What's to spy on?" asked Shelly. "One quick smooch. Big deal. I've seen more action on 'Sesame Street.'"

Annoyed, Stephanie told her, "I don't want you watching us. It's extremely rude."

"Relax," Shelly said. "I'll stop. It's either that or bore myself to death watching you and your dull life." Wrinkling her nose, Shelly marched into her room and shut the door.

Stephanie couldn't help feeling furious. Shelly had

been deliberately trying to goad her, she knew, but it hurt that she could do it so easily. *Am I really dull?* she found herself wondering.

She still hadn't made up her mind when she slipped between the sheets and turned out her light. In the darkness she felt all alone. No, she finally decided, her life wasn't dull. If anything, it was too eventful. David's death and then Kimberly's. The job and school pressures. Scott and her feelings for him. There was just too much going on, in fact, for her to cope with.

Her mind whirling with unresolved thoughts, she drifted to sleep.

When she woke again, she didn't know for a second what had roused her.

It was still very dark outside, and the street lights were still on; definitely the middle of the night. She hadn't been dreaming. As she lay quietly on her side, she glanced around her room. All the familiar shapes were there, vague in the gloom, but discernible. So what had woken her up?

It had been the sound of a click of some kind. Something snapping. Was there someone in her room? Worried, she lifted her head from the pillow and peeked around. There was no sign of anyone. Well, it had been a silly fear. She lay down again, trying to place the sound she'd heard. It was something familiar, something she heard before.

There was a vague sound of scratching. It seemed to be coming from the chair just inside her door. The one she'd dropped her bag on.

Her bag—*that* was the sound! It had been the snap lock on her purse!

She stared at the chair. Her bag was still there, lying on its side right where she had dropped it. Could someone have sneaked into her room and gone into her bag? It was the sort of thing that Shelly might be sneaky enough to try. Except that she was alone in her room.

The scrambling, scratching noise began again from her bag. It sounded like a mouse. Weird! Had a mouse managed to get into her room and crawl into her bag?

Right! A mouse that broke into purses! Some chance!

Still not willing to get up and check it out, Stephanie stared through the gloom at it. What was happening? She wasn't exactly scared, but she was definitely spooked.

A flash of light reflected off something at the edge of her bag, and then another scratching sound as something jumped down to the carpet.

She held her breath, her heart beating loudly. She could hear it pounding in her ears. There *had* been something in her purse! Slowly she peered over the side of the bed at the carpet where the thing had landed. In the faint light, she saw it glittering as it scrambled upright.

With sudden shock, she realized what she was staring at—the scarab brooch!

The brooch shook itself, finding its feet again in the thick pile of her carpet. It twisted its head to stare across at her bed. In the vague light Stephanie saw a glitter in the jeweled eyes.

*The thing was alive!*

She couldn't believe what she was seeing. Like a huge insect, the brooch was walking across the room toward her bed. Stunned, Stephanie simply watched the scarab make its way across the carpet. It was utterly impossible! She had held the brooch. It had definitely been made of silver and gemstones; it was not a living thing! How could it possibly be moving?

Now she realized why she'd heard her purse catch snap—she'd placed the brooch inside the coin section of her bag. The strange living creature it had become must have forced its way out.

No! This was crazy! She couldn't really be watching a possessed silver brooch crawl toward her bed. There had to be some explanation for this. There had to be!

Barely breathing, she couldn't take her eyes off the insectlike thing. There was another shiver of movement, and the pin beneath the body came free. The scarab somehow managed to curl the long, straight pin up across its back, like the stinger of a scorpion. When it was about a foot away from the bed, the scarab paused, as if gathering its strength. Then it leaped upward.

Stephanie gave a whimper as the thing landed on the edge of the bed. She sat up, staring down at the living brooch in horror. With an angry chittering noise, the scarab scuttled across the comforter. Stephanie brushed at it with her hand, trying to knock it to the floor. Hissing, the brooch stabbed her with the pin, whipping it like a tail.

A sharp pain slashed down across the back of her hand, leaving a trail of blood. Stephanie gasped, as much in shock as in pain.

*It was after her!*

Terrified, she threw the covers off her and over the thing. Then she jumped out of bed. There was a ripping sound as the scarab slashed its way out of the comforter using the pin. Tiny metallic legs levered it through the tear, and then it leaped at her again.

It landed on her shoulder and whipped the pin-stinger around. There was a sudden terrible pain below her collarbone as the scarab stabbed her. She gasped, tears welling up in her eyes, and stumbled. As she fell toward the floor, the brooch wrenched the pin free in a shower of blood and aimed the dripping weapon toward her eye.

Stephanie managed to twist her head. She felt the tip of the pin rip across her cheek, and then she fell onto the carpet. Stephanie's side ached from the fall, but the impact with the floor sent the brooch flying.

Groaning, she managed to roll onto her stomach. Her left shoulder was ablaze, and she could feel the blood trickling from the cut there. Her cheek hurt, but thank God the scarab hadn't got to her eye! She couldn't put any weight on her left arm, but she staggered to her knees using her right hand to push up from the floor. Then she stared around the room.

Where had the thing gone? She strongly doubted that it had given up. It seemed to be determined to kill her. She couldn't understand any of this, but now wasn't the time to try to figure it out. In the gloom, she couldn't see it at all. What she needed most was light, but the switch was across the room beside the door. It was only twelve feet, she guessed, but the brooch might be waiting for her to try for it.

This was crazy—trying to work out what a piece of jewelry was thinking! The scarab shouldn't be able to do any of this! Biting at her lip to prevent herself from whimpering, Stephanie started to rise to her feet. She was going to have to try to reach the light switch.

She saw a blur of motion, and tried to pitch herself aside. She wasn't quick enough. The scarab hit her thigh and slashed out with its pin-tail while clutching at her nightie. The material was too sheer, though, and it couldn't get a grip. The pin tore through the cloth, barely missing her leg. The brooch slipped, but the tail had enough purchase to avoid falling. As Stephanie swung around, she brushed at the scarab with her hand again. Using its tail to cling to her nightie, it couldn't stab her. But the six legs slashed her fingers. It was like getting six deep paper cuts at once. Stephanie couldn't help herself any longer—she screamed in pain.

She had to get the brooch off! Shaking at her nightie, she backed into her chest of drawers. The unexpected blow and her own gyrations to free herself made her stumble and fall.

This time the back of her head slammed onto the carpet, dazing her for a moment. The beetle sensed its advantage and clung to her, unaffected by the fall. As

Stephanie tried to get leverage with her right arm, the scarab scuttled across her nightie, up toward her chest. She thought it was making for her face again, but it skittered onto the skin between her breasts and swung the pin up again, rigid, ready to plunge it down.

*It was going to stab her through the heart!*

Her fingers connected with something on the floor. One of the shoes she'd kicked off earlier! She whipped it around, slamming it into the scarab as it was ready to strike. The unexpected blow sent it tumbling onto the carpet.

With a scream of fury and fear, Stephanie brought the shoe down on the brooch. The scarab kicked and tried to flee, but it was unbalanced. The shoe slammed it into the floor. She hit it again and again and again, panting and sobbing.

Her door crashed open and the light came on.

"Dear Lord!" exclaimed her mother, shocked. "Are you all right?"

Breathing heavily, Stephanie ignored the question. She pushed herself up to a sitting position, her shoe up and ready to strike again should it be needed. But the brooch was finished. It was no longer solid metal. Instead, it looked more like a small pile of tiny slivers of glass. . . .

It *was* no more than shattered glass. Unable to make any sense of this, Stephanie let the shoe fall.

Her mother was staring down at her, disbelief and concern waging war on her face. Stephanie groaned as she tried to sit up. She could only imagine what must be passing through her mother's mind, but Stephanie couldn't concentrate on anything except her injuries. Her left shoulder was still bleeding and painful. Her right hand had a deep cut across the back, and three of her fingers were dripping blood from the cuts. There was a streak of blood down her left thigh—she didn't even recall being cut there—and the side she'd fallen on felt like one massive bruise. Her nightie was shredded in several places where the brooch had attacked her, and her cheek and jaw were numb.

It was not going to be easy to explain any of this to her mother. Especially since she wasn't sure she could explain it to herself.

# CHAPTER 11

—➤

Stephanie winced as the hot water from the shower sent needles of spray into her aching body. She shifted around, to let it wash over her, cleaning off the dried blood, the antiseptic cream, and the sweat. Several times she had to clench her teeth to stop herself from screaming when the water hit a sensitive spot.

Her mother hadn't believed the story about the brooch coming to life, of course. Stephanie hadn't really expected her to. If someone had told that to her, she'd have laughed out loud. Mom had helped Stephanie to her feet, worry enabling her to avoid asking any further questions. Dad had wisely stayed in his room, assuming that the noise that had woken the family had been Stephanie having a bad dream and falling out of bed. Mom carefully let him believe this before locking herself in the bathroom with Stephanie.

"What *have* you been doing?" she had demanded, staring in horror at the wounds that covered Stephanie. "Is this some sort of self-mutilation?"

Stephanie had looked at herself in the full-length mirror on the back of the door. She looked even worse than she had imagined. "Do you think I'd do this to myself?" she asked. "This hurts like hell. I was *attacked.*"

"By an insect?" her mother asked, pulling out the first aid kit. "Sit down," she added. Stephanie sat on the toilet seat, trying not to wince as she did so. Mrs. Kirk had examined the wound on her shoulder. "That's not a bite," she remarked.

"It's a stab wound," Stephanie complained. "It wasn't an insect; it was a brooch."

That had been quite enough to convince her mother that Stephanie had been suffering from a very bizarre nightmare. She decided that *maybe* a real insect had run across Stephanie's skin during the vivid nightmare, and that had woken her up. As she spoke, trying to convince herself and Stephanie, she had worked at stopping the bleeding and treating the cuts.

"And how do you explain all these injuries?" asked Stephanie, annoyed that her mother wasn't even listening.

"You must have inflicted them on yourself."

Stephanie ouched as Mrs. Kirk rubbed antiseptic into her cheek. "Mom, I'd have to be *crazy* to do this!" When her mother didn't answer immediately, Stephanie became hurt. Mrs. Kirk avoided her gaze. Stung by this as much as by the real pain, Stephanie asked bitterly, *"Do* you think I'm crazy, then?"

"No!" her mother replied a shade too quickly and a shade too strongly. "I think you've been under a lot of stress, sweetheart. Your two friends dying. That dreadful job at the mall. Your schoolwork. Even your sister. I know Shelly can be a pain sometimes." She shrugged helplessly. "It was probably all just a bit too much for you."

Even now, early Saturday morning, this comment wounded Stephanie to the heart. Her mother had searched her room for anything to explain the cuts, but all she'd found was the small pile of glass shards that Stephanie had been pounding into the carpet. Stephanie realized that her mother must have believed that they were the wreckage of whatever Stephanie had used to cut herself. Stephanie knew better—and she also knew she wouldn't be able to prove it. She'd finally managed to get a little sleep, but was up early to take a shower.

She was hurting emotionally and physically. And none of this was making any sense.

When she felt that she'd washed away most of the ravages from the midnight attack, Stephanie set about washing her hair. It wasn't easy, because she had to work using only her right hand. Her left shoulder ached all the time, and when she tried to lift her arm it became a raging mass of pain that almost made her faint. The stab she'd received must have penetrated into the muscle. Even her right hand presented problems. She had Band-Aids around three fingers, and the cut across the back of her hand was painful and slightly inflamed.

She felt as if she'd been through a war—and maybe she had.

As she lathered the shampoo and then rubbed conditioner into her hair, Stephanie tried to figure out what had happened. There was only one explanation. She couldn't say it made sense, exactly. But it fitted the facts, which was all she demanded at that moment.

Dolman had tried to kill her, the way he had succeeded in killing Kimberly.

Stephanie knew it wasn't possible logically, but somehow that scarab brooch—an object made of silver and gems—had come to life and tried to murder her. It had possessed some malevolent intelligence, and if she hadn't woken up when it broke out of her purse, it might have found her sleeping and stabbed her through the heart before she woke up.

The comb Dolman had tricked her into taking to Kimberly must have done something similar. Just how Dolman could animate and give evil intelligence to a comb and a brooch she couldn't say, but she was utterly convinced that he had done it. And Kimberly's wild story about the mirror—suddenly didn't seem so wild. Dolman had provided it, and it had managed to drive David to attempted murder and Kimberly to the actual act.

Rinsing the conditioner out of her long blond tresses, Stephanie knew that there was absolutely no way to prove any of this. The scarab was—well, dead, she supposed. When she smashed it with her shoe, it had not broken into metal and precious stones but into thin slivers of glass. She'd carefully gathered up all of the shards and placed them in a sandwich bag that she'd hidden in her purse. She couldn't explain the transformation, but she remembered what Nicki had told her—that Kimberly had said the magic mirror shattered into shards of glass, too.

It was obvious that Dolman was trying to cover any tracks that might lead to him.

What wasn't clear was how he was doing it. And what she could do about it.

Telling the police was out. Mom had not believed the story about the brooch. Stephanie knew that even Nicki wouldn't accept it, let alone the law officers! And she couldn't think of anything that would make the police suspicious of Dolman. On the other hand, she couldn't just let him get away with what he had done—if for no other reason than that he might just try again to kill her. If he could animate a brooch, a mirror, and a comb, what might attack her next?

Would she be aware when an attack was coming?

No, she couldn't chance it. She *had* to settle with Dolman, and she had to do it that day. Fortunately it was Saturday—no school to cut. But she had to have a plan, some way of dealing with the disgusting old man . . .

Some way to gather proof that he was the cause of Kimberly's death and David's as well.

A confession? That would work. But how could she get one from him? He wasn't likely to volunteer.

Slowly as she brushed out her wet hair, an idea began to form in her mind.

Saturdays were always crazy at the mall. Stephanie and Nicki arrived early for their six-o'clock shift, but it took them five minutes to find a parking spot close enough so that they wouldn't have to spend the rest of the evening just walking to the restaurant. Once inside the mall, Stephanie realized that she had just twenty minutes to spare. Nicki was planning on shopping for a skirt before they started work, which fitted in well with Stephanie's plans.

"I'll see you there," she told her impatient friend. "I've got something to pick up at Dolman's."

"More important than new clothes?" asked Nicki with a laugh. "Okay. Just don't complain when I dazzle everyone and you don't." With a cheerful wave, she set off.

Stephanie headed down the crowded floor toward Dolman's store. *This is much more important than new clothes,* she thought. *I'm making sure I stay alive to wear them.* She had her tote bag slung over her shoulder, and she kept fingering the buttons on the small tape recorder she had inside it. She'd practiced, and could switch it on without glancing down. It was one of those pocket-size machines for dictating notes. Her father had used it for work, and she'd borrowed it from him. It was perfect for what she had in mind.

Dolman's seemed to have an invisible bubble about it that repelled the crowds of excited shoppers. People avoided even looking in the window. It was obvious that the old man wasn't making much money from this place. She had to wonder how he stayed in business, and what that business really was. Pushing the door open, she stepped into the familiar gloomy, dank room.

Stephanie had to force down the knot of fear in her stomach. Dolman had tried to kill her. Was it really smart of her to come alone into his store? But how else could she do it? Nicki would never have believed her, and Scott would have had her locked away. Until she had some kind of proof, she was forced to do this alone. But that didn't stop her from hating the task. Her heart thudded frantically as she passed by the antiques on display. How many of those might come alive at any second to attack her?

As she approached the counter, Dolman himself stepped out of the back room and glanced up to see who his customer might be. He stiffened and stared at her in shock—almost as much shock as was stamped on her own face.

He had clearly never expected to see her alive, and it was a moment before he recovered from the unpleasant surprise. It gave Stephanie the chance to fight back the incredulity that had seized her own mind.

*Dolman had changed!* He was no longer the gray-haired man in his late fifties she had seen the last time she'd entered this store. His hair was thick and dark, neatly cut and full. His face was slightly tanned, and most of his wrinkles were gone. He now appeared to be somewhere in his thirties. . . .

Which was completely impossible.

There was absolutely no doubt that it was the same man, not merely a younger relative who resembled him. Aside from the fact that he recognized her, he still had that same bad breath and odor of decay about him. His clothing was better, his shoes less scuffed. He looked like an average storekeeper instead of a dirty, tired old man.

She couldn't begin to imagine how this could have happened. It was merely one more impossibility in a whole mountain of them. She had to keep the upper hand here. She clicked on the tape recorder, then drew her hand out of the tote bag and held out the sandwich bag with the shards of glass in it. Not taking her eyes off him for a second, Stephanie dumped the bag out on the counter. Glass fragments tinkled out onto the dusty wooden surface.

"That's what's left of that scarab brooch you slipped into my bag," she told him coldly. "I thought you were trying to frame me for theft, but you weren't. You were trying to kill me, weren't you?" She had to avoid mentioning anything supernatural. If this tape was to be used as evidence, she had to sound completely rational!

Dolman swallowed hard, leaning on the counter for support. She was apparently the first person who'd survived his evil trap, and he was finding it hard to recover from his shock. "How—how did you—" He nodded at the glass pieces.

"I woke up," she told him. "You meant it to kill me while I slept." She pulled back her sleeve to show him the dressing on her shoulder, then touched the slash in her cheek. "It did try. It just wasn't good enough."

His eyes narrowed as he peered at her, trying to evaluate the extent of the disaster he had caused. "And now?" he asked her nervously.

"Now I want some explanations," Stephanie said. "How did you do this?" She waved at the glass splinters.

Dolman shivered, then seemed to find strength at last. "All right," he agreed. "I'll explain it all." He stepped back and gestured at the doorway to the inner room. "In here."

Suspiciously, Stephanie shook her head. "How stupid do you think I am? You've already tried to kill me once. If I go in there, you'll try again."

"I'm not a violent man," he protested. "I give you my word that I will not touch you or harm you in any way. But you won't believe anything I say unless you see it for yourself."

Stephanie considered this. She could well believe that he was a coward and wouldn't attack her. But all he needed to do was to stab her with one of his antique knives. On the other hand, would he chance doing anything here, when a customer might walk in at any second? She supposed that it depended on how desperate he was. Right now he seemed scared and uncertain rather than cunning and malicious. "Okay," she agreed reluctantly. "But you'd better not make any sudden moves."

"No, no," he assured her, leading the way into the other room.

As she entered, Stephanie saw that it was a workshop of sorts. At the far end stood a large table covered with jars and cans of wood preservatives, stains, and lacquers. That explained part of the dreadful stench, at least. Tools were scattered about, and an ancient chair stood on the table. He'd obviously been restoring it when she arrived.

The walls were lined with boxes and shelves. Most contained items in need of repair—chipped porcelain, items with splinters of wood missing, lamps needing rewiring, and furniture in dire need of refinishing. As in the outer room, the light here was very dim. There was a spotlight on the table, focused on the chair, and just a low-watt light in the ceiling that didn't illuminate much.

To one side of the room a small end table stood in front of a large, free-standing mirror. At least he said it was a mirror. She couldn't see the glass because it was covered with an old blanket. The mirror was about six feet tall, set in an ornately carved support that allowed the glass to pivot. She could make out only vague shapes carved into the dark wood, but they appeared to be twisted and somehow wrong. Dolman made straight for the mirror.

Standing on one side of it, he gave her a slight smile. "This is how it was done," he told her. "This mirror." He stroked the dark wood, his fingers caressing the oddly shaped designs carved into the wood.

"I don't get it," she admitted, moving slightly closer to get a better view.

"This is a very old mirror," he told her, his eyes starting to fill with obvious affection for the thing. She shuddered. It was creepy and somehow obscene. "I found it a long, long time ago," he went on. "And I have discovered that it is no ordinary mirror. It possesses *power.*"

"What sort of power?" Stephanie warily stared at the frame. She still couldn't make out any of the carvings, but they gave her a chill just the same. There was something about the thing that seemed to be . . . well, almost alive. It was as if the carvings were moving.

"The power to re-create," he said, almost in a whisper. "Haven't you ever looked into a mirror and thought that the reflection was so real you could almost reach into the glass and pluck it out?" He smiled. "Well, with this mirror, you *can.*"

"That's crazy," she protested, unable to take her eyes off the thing.

"No," he told her. "It's real. If I place anything on

154

this table, in front of the glass, then I can reach into the mirror and take out its reflection. That's what the brooch was—a reflection of a real brooch. That's why, when you broke it, your brooch reverted to its original substance—glass."

"Like the small mirror you sold Kimberly," whispered Stephanie. She didn't want to believe him, but the story did seem to explain some of the weird things that had been happening. . . .

"Exactly." Dolman nodded. "That was another reflection. So was the comb. If the mirror and the brooch hadn't been shattered, they would have returned to me, just as the comb did after it killed Kimberly. The real comb and mirror are on that shelf." He gestured to her right.

Before she even thought about it, Stephanie glanced up at the shelf he had indicated. Then, as he gave a cry of triumph and moved, she realized that he had tricked her. Expecting him to somehow attack her, she was completely unprepared for what he did do.

He threw back the blanket that was covering the mirror, carefully standing to one side of it.

Stephanie saw the pure glass reflecting the room back at her and, in the center of the mirror, an image of her own shocked face. Dolman was right—the mirror image *did* look real enough that she might be able to reach into the glass and pull something out.

Her heart pounded as she stared at her own reflection. There was something almost hypnotically enthralling about the image. She felt a thrill run through her skin like an electric shock as she stared into her own eyes. There was something terrible about this, something evil . . . Something very, very wrong.

Then she suddenly realized what it was that was twisted and out of place. She gasped as she looked at her reflection.

The image had a blood-red cut running down its right cheek—just as she did.

*The cut should have been on the left in a mirror image!*

Stephanie slowly raised her right hand. The image's right hand moved. Her skin crawled. Fighting down her panic, she tried to convince herself it was some sort of trick mirror, designed to show a reversed reflection. She didn't even begin to believe it. Her right hand touched her mouth in shock.

The image's right hand kept moving.

The reflection suddenly scowled at her, baring its teeth, and then lunged for her. Hands sprang out of the mirror as if emerging from water. One gripped her right hand; the other snatched a handful of her hair.

The reflection had come to life!

As she started to struggle, a scream welled up within her. Before she had a chance to let it loose, the image pulled sharply on her hand and hair, jerking her off-balance and pulling her forward into the glass.

Instead of slamming into a solid surface, she passed through the glass easily. The reflected Stephanie gave a cry of triumph and swung out of the mirror. In a whirl of motion, Stephanie was sucked into the glass while her image tore free and leaped into the real world.

Then Stephanie found herself looking out of the mirror-shaped entrance she had crossed, out into the room beyond.

Right into the eyes of her own reflection, which had taken her place! The eyes of her image were filled with hatred, disgust, and victory. . . .

# CHAPTER
# 12

~≫

Stephanie couldn't move. It was as if she were suspended in a thick fluid that was holding her in place. No matter how she strained, she couldn't flex a finger or turn her head or move her eyes. She was still breathing somehow, though *what* she was breathing she couldn't imagine. If she *had* been able to move, she knew she would have been shaking with terror.

Her reflection stared back at her, an unpleasant smile on its—*her!*—face. It was disturbing to see her own face focusing back on her with hatred and contempt. The mirror-Stephanie touched her face with her hands, lingering for a second on the cut on her cheek. Then she ran her hands down her neck, across her body, and down her stomach to her legs.

"Mmmm . . ." she purred. "I feel so *good.* If you'll pardon my choice of word." She was clearly talking to Dolman, not to Stephanie. "It really is rather delicious to have a body like this, isn't it?" She eyed Stephanie, appraising her. "And an attractive one at that. This is going to be a lot of fun for me, Dolman."

"Be careful!" Stephanie could hear Dolman's voice, even though she couldn't see him. He was staying well out of sight—for obvious reasons! The mirror could do everything he had claimed, including bringing her own image to some kind of unholy life.

The other Stephanie frowned. "Don't try to order me around, Dolman," she snapped.

"It's not an order," the dealer replied, attempting to placate the Stephanie-image. "It's just advice. You're not used to being alive yet."

"No," the mirror-girl agreed. "But I intend to get *very* used to it." She licked her lips. "I'm going to enjoy myself." Glancing at the mirror, she smiled. "Or *herself,*" she continued. "I can feel so many thoughts, so many sensations." She stroked the back of her left hand. "These human bodies are very sensitive, aren't they?"

"Yes," agreed Dolman. "And for that very reason, you must try to be careful. If you damage that body, you'll *hurt.*"

"You don't need to tell me that," the image answered. "I have all of *her* memories. I can remember the pain she felt last night." She touched her shoulder. "And I can still feel the pain in here. But it's not pain that I'm seeking—it's *pleasure.*" She turned and then paused. "Oh, yes." She stooped to lift Stephanie's tote bag. She had dropped it during the struggle. The other girl removed the tape recorder and switched it off. "You'll find this interesting, Dolman. She was taping the whole thing, ready to go to the police with it."

"Damnation!" Dolman sounded worried. "Did she—" He didn't finish the question.

"Her family didn't believe her. Surprise, surprise. The only other person she talked to is her friend Nicki." The mirror-Stephanie smiled. "And Nicki didn't believe her either. Still, if she causes any problems, I could always bring her down here, couldn't I? It might be fun to have a companion." She slung the bag over her shoulder. "Relax, Dolman. I'll make certain that nobody else disturbs you." As she walked out of the room, the image spun around and blew a kiss at the mirror. "So long, princess," she murmured. "Thanks for everything. I promise you I'll put it all to good use!" With a laugh, she walked out into the store. A moment later Stephanie heard the door to the shop open and then close.

She was gone—and Stephanie was trapped.

"What's happening?" she asked. She could speak, but it took a great effort. Her words were barely more than a whisper. She could see the frame of the mirror and the room beyond; it was like looking through a doorway. Everything on her side of the glass, though, was a gray nothingness—nothing to hear, smell, or see, except through the mirror opening.

"She's gone to replace you," Dolman told her. He stayed out of sight still. "Interesting little trick of yours, this tape recorder." She heard him place it on the table. "You're obviously very resourceful, young lady. It'll be helpful having you on my side from now on."

"How?" she asked. She couldn't manage more than a word or two at a time. Speaking took too much effort. She'd never be able to scream for help, even if there was some way to get her out of the mirror.

"I don't mind explaining," said Dolman. "You won't be getting out of there." She heard him settle down into the chair. "As I said, I discovered that this mirror could make copies of anything reflected in it. According to the former owner, this mirror was cursed. It created images that weren't quite right. Images that did not merely come to life; they also possessed life. The scarab brooch was one of them. When I made it, I instructed it to stay dormant until needed. Then it was to kill you. There's just a fragment of life in such images, since the originals have no life at all. But when the mirror duplicates a living thing, this effect is much enhanced.

"That image of you possesses all the memories and feelings that you have—and more besides. Part of the power within the mirror resides inside that duplicate. It's you—*plus*. Just as the brooch was a brooch until it attacked you. Just as the mirror that I sold Kimberly was just a mirror until she looked into it. And the comb was just a comb—until it cut her throat. That image of you is *exactly* like you, right down to the last hair. Even the parts of you that a mirror can't reflect are copied. If *you* have a birthmark, *she* has the same mark, in the same spot. If you had your appendix removed, then her appendix is gone."

"People . . . will . . . notice—" she gasped, more in hope than certainty.

"How?" he asked with a laugh. "She's *you*. She remembers everything you do. If you're allergic to roses, she's allergic to roses." He snorted. "She's not some stupid evil twin sister like in a bad movie. She's *you*."

"Not . . . me," Stephanie insisted. "Evil."

"Ah! You noticed that." Dolman chuckled. "Yes, the mirror does do that. It creates an image that is, shall we say, twisted? It's not a perfect copy in that sense. But let's face it—in all other aspects, she's you. It's just that she won't bother to hold back the darker side of your character." He laughed again. "In fact, she'll probably enjoy indulging it. But people will just think you've changed a bit. After all, given the sorry state of modern kids, what's a few more bad habits?"

Stephanie wasn't so sure that the duplicate would go undetected. But Dolman was right in many ways: people weren't likely to realize that the image was a fake. They would just think that Stephanie had changed, maybe because of the stress and strain of the past few days. She had a horrible feeling that the impostor might be able to fool everyone after all.

No, the image was not an impostor. That thing *was* Stephanie. It was a Stephanie that was warped.

Which left a very important question. "What . . . about . . . me?"

"You? Ah, now, that's not going to be to your

liking." Dolman stood up and began pacing back and forth nervously. She could hear him but could still not see him. "You obviously saw that I was younger when you came in. I saw the shock on your face right away. Well, let's say I have made a bargain with the mirror. It likes to cause destruction, and I give it the opportunity. It also enjoys killing people, absorbing their life. I give it that chance from time to time, as I did with David and Kimberly. Whenever someone dies as a result of the mirror, then the mirror absorbs that person's life force, the energies within that person. It thrives on its victims, feeding off them. And it siphons some of that force back to me. It enables me to become young again." He paused a moment. "How old do you think I am? I look thirty-five, don't I? Two days ago I looked fifty-five. A week ago I appeared to be seventy-five. Soon I could be twenty again." He paused again. "I was actually born in 1539, in Holland. Because of the power of the mirror, I'm actually in my mid–four hundred and fifties."

Stephanie felt another tingle of horror touch her skin. If she hadn't experienced everything she had, she would have thought him insane. Now it seemed only too possible. A mirror that created false images, feeding on its victims and keeping Dolman alive to ensure a steady stream of victims. But he still hadn't answered her question. "Me?" she repeated.

"As I said, when someone dies because of the mirror, it absorbs their energies." There was a definite relish to his words now. "You can't move, can you? You can't escape. You can't eat, or drink." What he was saying began to sink in with terrible force. Stephanie wanted to scream, but she couldn't. "You can't do anything," he told her. "Except die. That might take a couple of days. It might take a week, if you're really strong. But you'll die slowly, of thirst and starvation. Then the mirror will be able to absorb you." He laughed, a vindictive sound. "There's nothing you can do about it. Nothing at all."

Horror filled Stephanie. She struggled, trying to move, but the effort was useless. Her entire body was held invisibly but effectively. She was completely trapped, just as Dolman had said. Unable to move, like a fly in a spiderweb. All she could do was hang in place and slowly die of thirst. . . .

Her throat felt dry already. . . .

Nicki stowed her package in the employees' lounge of the restaurant. She could hardly wait to show Stephanie the neat new top she'd bought. She'd been looking for a skirt, but nothing had really struck her. Then she'd seen this incredible top and hadn't been able to resist it.

"Where's that lazy friend of yours?"

Looking up, Nicki saw Henry Blake standing in the doorway, using his hand to brush his thinning hair over his bald spot. Then she glanced at the time clock. "She's on her way," she told him. "She's still got five minutes, you know."

"She'd better be here," Blake snapped. "I'm getting tired of her behavior."

Nicki was stung by this incredible accusation.

"You're lucky she puts up with your crap," she told him. "I don't know anyone else who would."

"Yes," chimed in Paka, standing behind Blake. "You're just picking on her because she doesn't mouth off. You're trying to push that Stephanie, and one of these days she's likely to explode."

"That wimp?" Blake sneered. "She's shiftless, lazy, and a doormat. And the only thing you do with doormats is wipe your feet on them."

Furious, Nicki glared at him. "She's just too nice, that's her problem."

"Yes," agreed Paka again. "If Stephanie had any sense, she'd stick that broom right up where it belongs."

"Aren't you both supposed to be working?" asked Blake, coloring. "Or would you like me to dock your pay?"

Before either of them could answer him, the door down the hall opened, and Stephanie entered. She was a little flushed as if she'd been running, and there was an almost giddy expression in her eyes.

"You're late, Kirk," Blake snapped.

Stephanie shook her head slightly as if coming back in for a landing from space. Then she flicked her eyes over to the clock. "What's wrong, Henry?" she asked. "Haven't you learned to tell time yet? I've still got four minutes."

Nicki was amazed at her friend's reply, but not half as astonished as Blake. "What?" he screeched. "Don't give me any of your lip."

"Then keeps yours buttoned," Stephanie advised.

Pushing past the three of them, she retrieved her time card and punched in. "There," she said, waving it under his nose. "I'm on time, right?"

"Then get to work," Blake spluttered. "You're on cleanup duty."

"Am I?" Stephanie turned and stared at him. Blake shifted uncomfortably. "I seem to recall I've been on garbage duty all week. I've had enough."

Blake was ready to explode. Nicki hoped he had a strong heart, because otherwise he'd have an attack. "Don't tell *me* you've had enough!" he squeaked furiously.

Abruptly, Stephanie's hand shot out. She grabbed the front of Blake's shirt, spun him around, and slammed him against the wall. "Listen you creep," she snarled. "You'd better change your tone. I'm sick of you, and I'm not going to suck up to you any longer. Get it?"

"Let go of me!" Blake whined. "This is assault. I'll fire you for this!"

"You don't need to fire me," Stephanie said. "I quit. I don't work for emotionally backward jerks like you. But before I go, I'll do one last bit of garbage detail." Before anyone else could move, she whirled Blake around again. His squeal of shock and fear was cut off as Stephanie shoved his head into the nearest trash container. "There. You must feel right at home."

Nicki stared at her friend, slack-jawed. She couldn't believe what she was seeing. Stephanie had never acted like this before. Paka appeared to be just as stunned. Stephanie gave them both a big wink, then blew a kiss in the direction of Blake. He'd pulled himself out of the trash can and was spitting out coffee grounds and wiping the garbage from his face.

"Bye-bye, Henry," she purred, and she marched down the corridor and out of the restaurant.

Nicki just stared. The door opened again a second later. Henry whimpered, obviously afraid that Stephanie had come back again. It was just her cap, however, thrown over her shoulder like a Frisbee. The door slammed shut once more.

Glancing at Blake, Nicki couldn't help giggling. He looked dreadful. "Henry," she murmured, "you need a bath."

Spluttering and blazing red with embarrassment, Henry slid off toward the employees' bathroom. Nicki suspected he'd be in there for most of her shift.

Paka gave Nicki a very bemused look. "I know I told her she had to be more assertive," she said. "But what got into *her?*"

# CHAPTER

# 13

~

Scott was still attempting to sort out his feelings for Stephanie. She'd just called him and asked him to pick her up at the mall. She hadn't explained why she wasn't working, but she'd insisted that she needed a ride. He'd agreed to provide one. Now, as he drove, he worked at understanding what she meant to him.

He was still more than a little sore about the previous night. He'd done nothing more than put his hand on her knee, and she'd read him the riot act. Surely they'd been going together long enough for her to be a little more romantic? It wasn't as if he'd made a pass at her or anything. She was just overreacting.

He couldn't hide behind the anger too long, however. He was too honest for that. If she hadn't stopped him, he knew he would have gone further. Stephanie was right in one way—that could be the end of their relationship. She'd been honest from the beginning with him; she'd told him that she didn't care what other girls did—*she* didn't. And wouldn't. She'd been happy enough to share kisses, but that was all. It was very frustrating for him, especially when the other guys on the team bragged about scoring.

But . . . Well, to be honest, he preferred dating Stephanie to scoring with any other girl. She was really special, and he suspected that part of her appeal for him was that she didn't fool around. He always knew exactly where he stood with her.

Unfortunately, it was always outside the door.

The problem was, he knew, that he wanted it both ways: he wanted Stephanie, just as she was. And he also wanted her to change her mind about sex. He was constantly wavering between the two conflicting desires.

He'd deal with it. Not easily, maybe, but he would.

Stephanie was waiting for him by the entrance to the mall, as she'd promised, and she climbed into the car beside him as he stopped. She seemed a little different somehow, but Scott couldn't put his finger on why. She'd probably changed her hair or bought a new skirt or something, and she'd be all upset if he didn't notice! There was a cut on her cheek, but he didn't like to ask about it. Stephanie could be a bit vain at times, and wouldn't want to be reminded of it. "You're out early," he said.

"I quit," she told him, giving him an almost hungry look. "I couldn't take it any more."

"About time," he replied. Yet he couldn't help being puzzled, because she had never given him any indication in the past that her job was that dreadful. Oh, well! He turned the car around and headed toward the Kirk house. "So what are you going to do now?"

She gave him one of her dazzling smiles. They always made him feel mushy. "Enjoy myself," she told him.

"Nice work, if you can find it," he joked.

"I can find anything I want," she assured him. He could believe it.

The small talk petered out fast, but so did the trip. It was just turning dusky when he pulled up outside the Kirk house. He switched off the engine and gave her a grin. "Anything else I can do for you?" he asked.

"Yes," she replied, leaning over toward him. "Lots more." She gave him a long, very hungry kiss. Scott reacted in kind, and she pressed closer.

Much closer. Scott could feel his pulse racing and his body going into overdrive. Stephanie was definitely hot! His back pressed against the door as she almost climbed onto him. She ran her hand down his chest, setting him afire.

"Mmm," she purred, gently nibbling at his ear.

"You taste good." Her eyes sparkled. "And you feel good, too." She was panting slightly, and when he stared into her eyes they were so wide he was afraid he'd fall into them and drown. She certainly set him reeling! She bent down again for another long kiss, and he clutched her close. He could smell the perfume in her hair as she buried her face in his.

With a jerk, he pulled away from her. "Hey!"

Stephanie had leaned forward so far that she was almost overbalanced. She was forced to let him go and grab the headrest. Her left knee was on the passenger seat, exposing much more of her long, shapely leg than he felt safe seeing. "What's wrong, lover?" she murmured.

Confused and shaken, Scott stammered, "I-I thought you said . . . last night—"

"I've changed my mind since then," she replied, licking her lips and staring at him.

"You said that sex was out," he reminded her. He felt terribly hot and uncomfortable.

"I told you I changed my mind," she purred. "Isn't that what you wanted?"

*Yes!* he thought, but at the same time he forced himself to shake his head. "That's what I thought," he admitted. "But now I'm not sure."

A spark of anger kindled in her eye. "What's wrong, lover? Are you chicken?"

"It's not that," he told her honestly. "God knows, I'd love to—" He shook his head. "But this just isn't *you*, Steph."

She raised her chin, definitely annoyed now. "Can't take a woman who knows what she wants and isn't afraid to go for it?" she snapped.

"I'm not sure that this is what you want," Scott replied. He gave her a hard look. "You've never acted like this before."

"I've never wanted you like this before," she said. "Don't you *prefer* me like this?"

"No," he told her. To his astonishment he realized that this was perfectly true. He didn't want Stephanie as a sex object. "I prefer you the way I've always known you. What's wrong with you?" he asked her, concerned. "Do you feel all right?"

"I feel fine," she told him, tossing her head. *"You're* the one with the problem."

"This just isn't you, Steph," he said again. "You're acting weird."

"Well, you're not the only fish in the sea!" she cried furiously, straightening up in her seat. "If you don't want me, I'll find someone who does!"

"Stephanie," Scott begged her, "please! Listen to yourself! This isn't like you at all. You're scaring me."

"I'll do more than scare you," she spat out. She slammed open the car door. "You had your chance and you blew it, jerk." She slid out of the car and glared at him. "Take one last good look at me, Berman." Her lip curled into a sneer. "And think about this: you could have had me, and now somebody else *will.*" A thought obviously crossed her mind, and she smiled cruelly. "And that some-body will be Brent Wardlow." She tossed her head back again. "Think about *that*—and weep." She whirled around and took off up the path to her house.

Shaking, Scott watched her march inside and slam the door behind her. Then he collapsed over the steering wheel, on the edge of tears.

What had he done? Had he really lost her? And for what? For refusing to do what he most wanted! It was crazy!

No.

*She* was crazy.

Scott straightened up and stared at her house. This wasn't the Stephanie he knew. There had to be something seriously wrong with her for her to behave like this. Maybe this was a reaction to all she'd been through in the past few days. Maybe the death of David and Kimberly had made her think she had to live fast and furiously, in case she was fated to die soon, too.

He didn't know what was wrong with her; that was the problem. He punched the dashboard, hurting his hand. He couldn't imagine what was going through her mind. He had to talk about this with somebody. Get advice. But from whom? Her parents were out of the question. He could just imagine what their reaction would be if he told them their daughter had tried to seduce him. Same problem with his own parents.

Nicki! He could talk to her. She was Stephanie's best friend. If anyone could help him, she could. Maybe she'd noticed something odd about Stephanie, too. Together they might be able to help her.

He started the car and turned it around to head back to the mall. All he could hope was that Stephanie hadn't really meant what she'd said about Brent Wardlow.

Shelly knelt on her bed, staring out through the blinds, shocked. She couldn't believe what she was seeing! Her goody-goody older sister was all over Scott Berman! Eyes bulging, Shelly watched through the slats. This was going to be great!

To her disappointment, the two in the car seemed to have an argument. Then Stephanie jumped out and slammed her way into the house. Shelly licked her lips in anticipation. Boy, this was fun! She had the goods on her two-faced, holier-than-thou sister now! All that talk about being good was so much crap. She heard Stephanie storm into her room and throw her bag down on the chair. Then she wandered across the hall and stared in at her big sister.

Stephanie was standing in the middle of her room taking deep breaths, her fists clenched and her eyes closed. She seemed really ticked off. Shelly smiled. Perfect! "Had a bad day?" she asked in mock sympathy.

Her sister's eyes opened and focused on her. Shelly was chilled by the look she was given. There was pure hatred in Stephanie's eyes, something she had never seen before. "Get lost," Stephanie hissed.

For a moment Shelly considered doing exactly that. Then her finely tuned instinct for blackmail kicked in, and she smiled at her older sister. "I saw what you were doing with Scott," she sneered. "I'll just bet Mom and Dad would love to hear how you were groping him in the car."

Before Shelly could move, Stephanie had whirled around. Her right hand shot up, fastening itself around Shelly's throat and shoving her back against the wall. Shelly gave a cry of shock and pain as her back connected with the plaster. Lowering her head, Stephanie stared into Shelly's eyes.

"I told you to stop spying on me," she said coldly. "I'm not going to tell you again. One word from you to our folks and I'll beat the living daylights out of you."

Shelly felt a knot of fear growing inside her. Despite this, she still managed to say, "You wouldn't dare!"

"Wouldn't I?" Stephanie appeared to consider the question for a second, then lashed out with her other hand and punched Shelly in the stomach. Shelly gagged, and would have fallen if the hand around her throat hadn't been holding her upright. As she wheezed in agony, Stephanie shook her. "You want to reconsider that threat?" she asked sweetly. Then she let Shelly go.

Shelly fell to the floor, her stomach on fire. She

stared up at her older sister, tears in her eyes. "I didn't mean anything," she whimpered.

"You'd better not mean anything," Stephanie said. "Now get lost. I've got things to do." She pointed a finger at Shelly. "And if you say one word about this to Mom and Dad, you'll wish you hadn't. Do you understand?"

Nodding, Shelly staggered to the door. "Not a word," she gasped. "I promise."

"Good." Stephanie turned her back on her sister and started to unbutton her blouse. "Shut the door behind you," she ordered.

Shelly did so. She made her way back to her room and collapsed on her bed. She touched her stomach carefully. She felt awful. That had been a vicious punch, with plenty of venom behind it. What could have gotten into Stephanie? She'd never behaved like that before. She just wasn't herself. . . .

Scott tried to sort out what was going through his mind as he drove around, killing time until Nicki would be done working. Not all of it made sense to him, but it was quite clear that something was very wrong with Stephanie. Her wild behavior was way off base. The gentle, caring person he had grown to care about had suddenly become a predatory creature, violent and voracious. The only explanation that came to his mind was that she must have been having a nervous breakdown of some kind after all she'd been through.

Did she really mean what she'd said about Brent? Or was that just another vicious dig to try to hurt him? The thought of her with another guy—*any* other guy, let alone that sleazeball Wardlow!—really ate at him. He couldn't rid his mind of the picture of her offering herself to Brent. It was burning him up.

He arrived back at the mall ten minutes before closing. Nicki couldn't get off till the cleaning was finished. Every second he waited seemed like a day, and every minute was filled with terrible images of what Stephanie might be doing. Finally he could stand it no longer. He went to a pay phone and dialed the Kirks' number.

Mrs. Kirk answered. Scott hesitated. What could he ask her without getting Steph in trouble? As soon as he identified himself, however, Mrs. Kirk gave a cry of relief.

"Scott! Is Stephanie with you?"

"Uh, no, she isn't," he replied, trying to keep the alarm from his voice. "Why? What's happened?"

"Shelly said Stephanie came in acting strange and then went out about an hour ago without saying where she was off to or when she'd be back." The worry in Mrs. Kirk's voice was very obvious. "Simon and I arrived home just a little while ago, and we have no idea where she is. We hoped she was with you or Nicki."

There was no point in lying. It wouldn't help matters at all. "She's not with either of us," he told her. "I'm waiting to see Nicki right now." There was a cold knot of pain and fear in his stomach. "Look, I do have an idea where she might have gone. We'll swing around there and look for her. If we don't find her, I'll give you a call, okay?"

"Where do you think she is?" Mrs. Kirk demanded.

"Uh, I could be wrong," Scott told her. "I'll be in touch, I promise." He slammed down the phone before she could ask any more questions. Then he stared at it, breathing hard and feeling giddy. *She did it,* he thought. She'd really gone to Brent's.

He'd waited long enough. If Nicki wasn't ready now, he'd leave without her. He ran back to the Burger Heaven exit, arriving just as the employees were leaving. Henry Blake, looking somewhat more subdued than normal, was setting the alarm. Nicki waved and came to meet Scott.

"Come on," he said, grabbing her hand.

"Hey!" she cried, trying to tug herself free. "What's wrong? Where are we going?"

"After Stephanie," he told her. "I'm afraid she's in real trouble."

Nicki stopped struggling and came with him. "What sort of trouble?" she asked.

"I don't know exactly. I'll explain on the way." They had reached his car now. Nicki glanced back across the parking lot to where her own vehicle sat.

"What about my car?" she asked.

"I'll drive you back in the morning to get it," he

snapped. "Isn't helping Stephanie more important right now?"

Nicki chewed at her lower lip, undecided, then nodded. "Yeah, okay." She slipped into the passenger seat, and Scott started the engine and then roared away. "So where are we going?" she begged. "What's happened to Steph?"

Scott concentrated on driving as fast as he dared. It wouldn't do to be stopped by a cop for speeding, but he was desperate to get to Brent's house. As he drove, he explained what had happened earlier.

Nicki stared at him in amazement. "*Stephanie* did that?" she asked. "You've got to be kidding!"

He smiled without any humor. "I wish I was," he told her. "It was just so unlike her."

"Yeah." Nicki's eyes widened. "And you turned the offer down flat? Boy, that must have taken some doing."

"It did," he admitted. He gave her an agonized glance. "I almost wish I hadn't. But—well, if she's sick, it wouldn't have been fair of me to accept, would it?"

Nicki shrugged. "No, I guess not. But I doubt if that kind of distinction will bother Brent much. He's used to taking what he wants when he wants it. And if Stephanie really is going there, then there's no way he'll turn her away."

"Don't you think I know that?" Scott asked. There was real pain in his voice. "The thought of what he might do is tearing me up."

Nicki nodded sympathetically. In her own mind, the idea of Stephanie offering herself to Brent Wardlow was the second most repugnant thing she could imagine.

The most repugnant, of course, was what would happen when he accepted. . . .

# CHAPTER

# 14

~

Brent sat on the couch in front of the TV, his feet on the coffee table, and took another swig of the beer he'd swiped from the fridge. He wasn't really sure what he was watching, as this was his fourth can, but he felt good anyway. As he put the can down, he belched.

His mother had gone out for the evening with her latest boyfriend, so Brent had the house to himself. His father had gone out for the evening six years earlier and never returned. He was living somewhere in Florida. Brent didn't miss him—the regular beatings he'd suffered as a kid had stopped when his father left. Now it was Brent who dealt out the blows. He'd never be picked on again.

The doorbell rang. Brent ignored it and took another pull on the beer. It rang again. The idea of getting up from the couch didn't appeal to him. It was probably just one of the neighbors come over to complain about the volume of the TV again. When the bell rang for the third time and kept on ringing, he swore and stumbled to his feet. Weaving around the furniture, he made his way to the door. Whoever was ringing the bell was really ticking him off. He jerked open the door and stared at the girl on the doorstep. It took him a moment to recognize her.

"Hi, Brent," Stephanie purred, her eyes scanning him all over.

"What the hell do you want?" he snapped. Now he knew who she was—Scott Berman's girl. But she lived a mile or so away, he thought. She obviously wasn't here to ask him to turn down the TV.

"You," she replied.

Brent's eyes narrowed as he stared at her. She was wearing a tight top that accentuated her figure and a skirt that barely seemed long enough to avoid being called a belt. She had great legs, and he had to tear his gaze away from them to look at her face. "What for?"

"Oh, I don't know," she murmured. "Let's improvise, shall we?" Without waiting to be asked, she pushed his arm away from the door and sauntered inside.

Brent watched her, bewildered. She didn't seem to be here to complain about Brent beating up on her guy. So why was she here? The screen door banged shut, so he left the front door open as he followed her.

He might want to kick her out on her shapely back-side.

Stephanie picked up the beer can and shook it. Then she tipped it up and finished it off. She let the empty can fall to the carpet, then turned to face him. There was froth on her lips, and she licked it off, not taking her eyes off him for a second. She was really one cute babe, and Brent felt a stirring of interest inside him. Or was it gas?

She glanced at the TV, then grinned. "Is that all you had planned for the evening?" she asked.

"It's better than nothing," he answered.

Stephanie switched it off. In the sudden silence she gave him a dazzling smile. "I have something in mind that's better than *anything*," she told him. As he gave her a puzzled look, she moved in closer, her lips slightly parted. Then she raised her arms, slipped them around his neck, and pulled him closer for a long, passionate kiss.

It electrified Brent. He'd had girlfriends before—though never for long—but none of them had ever kissed like *this*. It seemed to set him tingling from his hair to his toenails. As she let him go, he took in a huge gulp of air. Her behavior didn't make any sense to him, but there was no way he was going to complain about it.

"I thought you were Scott Berman's girl," he said.

"Emphasis on *was*," she told him, her face only six inches from his. He couldn't take his eyes off her—and didn't want to.

That made him feel good. Yeah—it made sense. Why would she want a wimp like Berman when she could have *him?* He grinned, then grabbed her, pulling her in for a kiss this time. His head was spinning—possibly from the beer, possibly from her. He didn't care which.

Then there came the sound of a car pulling up outside. Brent had to force himself to break off the kiss. Of all the bad times for his mom to come home! Then he frowned. That wasn't his mom's car. It didn't belong to anyone he knew, even though it was parked right outside the house. Stephanie didn't seem bothered by its arrival. He tried to concentrate on her, but movement from the car made him look through the mesh of the screen door again. Two people emerged from the car, and he recognized them both: Scott Berman and Nicola Powers.

Stephanie's boyfriend and her best friend . . .

Anger welled up inside him. It was all so obvious to him now! He understood clearly why Stephanie had come on to him like this. The slut was setting him up so that when Scott arrived the jerk would have an excuse to waste him. And with that Powers girl as a witness that Scott was provoked!

"You—" he snarled, pushing her away from him. Anger was burning in his stomach now. Nobody made a fool out of Brent Wardlow without paying in blood. "You set me up!"

Stephanie half turned and saw who was approaching the door. Then she bared her teeth and hissed. "Damn them!"

Rage consumed Brent. He grabbed a handful of her long hair. She gave a cry of pain, which made him feel better. He twisted the knot of hair to get a better grip, dragging her closer. She gasped again, tears filling the corners of her eyes. This was better than sex anyway. "You're gonna pay for trying to make a fool out of me," he promised. Then, venting all of his anger into the one motion, he spun about, dragging her by the hair, and slammed her into the wall as hard as he could.

"Is this the place?" Nicki asked as Scott turned off the engine. It was quite a nice-looking little house, set about twenty feet back from the road. She'd expected Brent to live in a roach motel or somewhere similar.

"According to the phone book, yeah." Scott's fists clenched the steering wheel. "There's someone home." He didn't have to ask the obvious.

"Then let's visit," suggested Nicki, unfastening her seat belt. "Come on."

He nodded, and they got out of the car together. Scott was holding back, and Nicki couldn't blame him. She knew he dreaded going up to the door. If Stephanie wasn't here, they'd both look like fools. And if she *was* here? Then what? Nicki clenched her teeth, refusing to consider that possibility. Stephanie needed help, that was obvious. Without checking to see that Scott was following, she marched up the pathway.

The front door was open, though the screen door wasn't. Through the mesh, Nicki saw two people inside, locked in what she would definitely have had to call a close embrace. The guy was Brent, and the girl—with her back to the door—had long, blond hair. It *had* to be Steph! Nicki's heart sank. How could she be so stupid as to come here? If she was gutter-hunting, there had to be other human dregs to pick. But none, she knew, that would hurt Scott more.

As she moved up the pathway, Nicki saw Brent push the blond girl away. The girl turned—there was no doubt that it was Stephanie—and then said something. Brent grabbed a handful of her hair, and Steph screamed.

Nicki ran the rest of the way as fast as she could. She heard Scott's feet pounding behind her. They both reached the screen door as Brent swung Stephanie around and started to smash her face against the wall.

Nicki anticipated the pain. Steph's face was going to be a horrible mess from that—

Instead of a thump, though, as flesh hit the wall, there was a loud crash, like that of a brick going through a plate-glass window. Nicki howled.

Stephanie's head shattered into a thousand shards of glass. Then her body did the same. The hair in Brent's hands turned to razor-sharp needles of glass. The sound of the explosion as Stephanie fragmented drowned out Nicki's incoherent scream and Brent's howl of mortal terror. The slivers of glass exploded outward from the impact point as if a bomb had detonated. They ripped through everything in their path, then slammed into the carpet, the ceiling, and the walls.

Nicki couldn't tear her eyes away from the horrible sight. Scott could, and did. She vaguely heard him retching and throwing up on the lawn. Forcing her own bile down, Nicki clutched at the screen door for support as she saw Brent collapse.

He'd been slashed and pierced by hundreds of the needles of glass. Small slivers and larger knifelike chunks had been driven into his body. He must have died instantly. Not one inch of his body remained untouched.

Nicki collapsed, shaking, onto the stoop. She couldn't imagine anything so horrific. Seeing the bullets rip into David had been bad enough—but this was beyond comprehension! Stephanie had shattered into lethal shards of glass—

Not like a human being. Like a mirror . . .

Forcing herself not to think about Brent's broken, bleeding body, Nicki suddenly realized that the girl hadn't been Stephanie at all. It had been something that looked like her. A thing made of animated glass, not flesh and blood. A thing that had exploded when Brent slammed it into the wall.

Nicki took several deep breaths, striving to regain control of her stomach and her sanity. When she was certain she could move without fainting, she staggered drunkenly to her feet. Scott was lying on the lawn, pale and weak.

"Come on," she told him. "There's nothing we can do here." As she forced herself to move, she felt control of her body returning. Her mind was already blotting out what she'd witnessed.

187

"Stephanie," he groaned as he sat up. He fumbled in his pocket for a tissue, then wiped his mouth.

"That wasn't Stephanie," she told him grimly. That much was clear to her now. All the time she'd made fun of Steph for believing Kimberly, but Steph had been right. "It was some kind of solidified reflection."

"What?" Scott stared at her, utterly lost, as she helped him to his feet.

"A mirror image," she said. "Her exact twin, but not a real double. Just an image made of glass. That's why she exploded like that."

"I don't understand," he told her.

"Neither do I, really," she admitted. "But it's starting to make sense. I'll explain on the way."

"On the way where?" He managed to follow her as she headed for the car, but his mind was still focused on what he'd witnessed.

"Back to the mall," Nicki said. "To Dolman's. Stephanie told me she was going there, and she changed right after she did. Now I know why." She saw the confusion in his eyes. "I'll explain on the way." Scott was in no shape to drive. "Keys," she demanded, holding out her hand. Without protest, he gave them to her. "I'll drive."

"But what about Brent?" he asked. "Shouldn't we check first?"

"There's no need," she informed him. Frozen in her mind was his face, with a large shard of glass buried deep inside it and emerging from the back of his head. "He's dead." She shuddered, forcing the memory from her thoughts. "Let's go. We've got to find Stephanie—the *real* one!"

Stephanie tried to focus her mind, but it was getting more and more difficult for her to think of anything but the burning in her throat and the need for something to drink. She knew that she'd been in this nothingness for five or six hours max, but she felt as if she'd been there forever. A haze was settling over her mind, and apart from her terrible thirst she couldn't feel her body at all.

Dolman had thrown the cover back over the mirror several hours before, so there wasn't even anything outside the gray bleakness for her to concentrate on. The mall had to be closed by now. Would she be able to sleep? Or would she stay awake for the whole period? Her throat hurt so badly now. What would it be like after a night here?

Vague shadowy images were running through her mind. Kind of like memories, but not hers. At first she'd thought they were hallucinations brought on by her suffering, but then she realized that she was somehow tapped into the mirror-Stephanie. The mirror image had stolen her memories and form, so she wasn't shocked to discover that she could vaguely hear her image's thoughts. They were very whispery and easily drowned out, but with nothing else to occupy her mind, Stephanie strained to follow what was happening.

She could vaguely feel the desires of her other self.

The other Stephanie had stood up to Henry Blake and humiliated him. It wasn't what Stephanie would have done, but it was what she'd *wanted* to do. The image had then come on to Scott. Well, she felt the same attraction, and if she hadn't cared so much about the consequences of her actions, she might have given in to him long ago. And as for setting Shelly straight, the image had done it with needless violence, but Stephanie could easily have given in to that urge herself!

The difference was that Stephanie cared about other people and understood that such behavior was wrong. The image simply didn't think about right or wrong; it did whatever it wanted to do. It had no worries about the consequences of its actions. There was no thought behind its behavior.

And as for going to see Brent Wardlow! The boy sickened her. How the image could contemplate it escaped Stephanie. The mirror-Stephanie had simply wanted to strike back at Scott and hurt him. The savagery of the reflection was astonishing. If Stephanie ever did get free from this mirror, what would everyone think of her? Surely Scott thought she was a tramp, Shelly thought she was a bully, and Nicki thought she was crazy. And what about Brent? She was vaguely aware of Brent grabbing her double and then slamming it against the wall.

Suddenly everything became intensely real again. The gray nothingness vanished in a huge wave of pain that pierced every atom of her being. With a scream, Stephanie pitched forward. For a brief second something resisted her, and then she toppled forward through the blanket covering the mirror and landed on the floor.

She lay there, stunned and hurting. Pins and needles flashed through her body as the feeling started to return. Her cheek was hurting from the fall, as was her right shoulder, which had taken most of the blow.

It felt wonderful.

Just to be alive and somehow free of the mirror! She'd put up with all of the pain and discomfort, but now she was free! Slowly she breathed in and out, trying to recover her wits. Her image had been destroyed, and that had catapulted her back from that gray void into the real world again.

Then she felt a stab of fear: would the mirror be able to copy her again? Would another image draw her back inside? Refusing to surrender to her pain, Stephanie managed to turn her head and look back at the mirror.

The blanket was a bit lopsided from her fall, but it still covered the mirror. She was safe! She let loose a huge sigh of relief, and that made her aware of her terrible thirst again. Her throat was on fire now. She had to quench it somehow. The mirror had drained the strength out of her, as if it had been sucking the life from her. It had intensified her thirst to an unbearable degree.

It wasn't safe to touch anything in this store. She had to get to one of the water fountains in the mall. Gathering the shreds of her strength, she sat up. Dizziness almost forced her to lie down again, but she fought it. Gradually the screaming in her ears and head died down to a buzz. The glaring red haze across her eyes retreated. She took several deep breaths, then staggered to her feet.

A wave of nausea swept over her, and she stumbled into the wall beside the door. Gripping the frame, she managed to lock her fingers around the doorjamb and support herself. The pain began to ebb a little. Her head stopped threatening to explode. After a few minutes she could focus her attention on getting out of the room. She was still weak and didn't even want to begin cataloging all of the aches and jagged pains she was forcing down. Carefully, she released her grip on the frame and stood upright.

She couldn't help swaying a little, but she felt fairly confident that she could manage to walk without falling down. Taking it slowly, Stephanie stumbled through the main part of the shop. It was dark inside the store even when the lights were on. Now, at night, it was impossible to see anything but vague shapes. The lights in the mall would be dimmed, she knew, but there would be lighting of some kind. And there was a night guard who patrolled. She could get help—but first she had to get water.

Concentrating on that, she made her way through the store. In the gloom everything took on a sinister appearance, especially the two suits of armor. She almost expected them to come to life and attack her. But nothing happened.

She reached the door and through the glass could see the mall outside. There was sufficient illumination for her to make out the lock. Her fingers still throbbed with pins and needles, but she managed to unlatch it on the third attempt and then pulled the door open. She didn't bother closing it when she staggered outside.

Stephanie didn't look back. Her attention was focused on getting to the food court. There were bathrooms there with water fountains. Cool, wonderful water . . .

In the darkness behind her, there was a slight movement, which she hardly noticed. An ancient brass lectern stood near the entrance to the store, a large stand, over four feet tall, made in the shape of an eagle with outspread wings to support a book on its back. As Stephanie started down the empty corridor, the eagle's eyes snapped open, two bright, burning metallic eyes. Then the eagle shuddered and burst free from its stand.

# CHAPTER
# 15

Groaning, Dolman awoke. He gazed at his alarm clock. It was barely midnight, and yet a voice in his mind was telling him to get up. Maybe it was just a bad dream?

Then he sat upright as the whispered thought grew stronger. It was the mirror. Something had gone wrong! Linked to it as he was, Dolman could feel the urgency of the call. The eagle lectern he'd left guarding the shop entrance had woken up. It was crying out to the mirror, and that in turn had wakened Dolman.

He leaped from the bed and switched on the light. He saw the lines and liver spots on his hand and knew the rest. He was aging again, which meant that somehow that accursed girl had gotten free! As he hastily pulled on his clothing, he realized that the mirror-Stephanie was gone. It had not understood the need to control its passions. It had somehow provoked its own destruction, and that had sent the real girl back out of the mirror and started his aging again.

Well, she was still trapped inside the mall. And Dolman lived only five minutes away. All he had to do was reach her before she got away. He could use the mirror to send his messengers after her. This time she wouldn't escape.

Even if the eagle didn't get her, she was doomed.

It was the longest journey of Stephanie's life. She leaned on the plate-glass windows for support as she made her way down the hollow, empty hallway toward the rest rooms. The low-level lighting made the place ghostly. The shops all stood as they did during the day, but without people around, the mall was one vast graveyard.

Silly thoughts! Pushing them to the back of her mind, Stephanie almost collapsed as she pushed her way through the door of the women's room and went inside. She gasped with relief as she saw the water fountain and staggered the rest of the way to it. Her shaking fingers held down the button that operated it. Water arced out, and she thrust her face into the stream. Gulping down the cold, wonderful liquid, she felt the fire in her throat and belly die and vanish. Still she greedily sucked in more water until her thirst was slaked. Her face and hair were dripping wet, but she didn't care.

Feeling marvelously refreshed, she finally straightened up. Throwing her hair back, she felt cold water splatter down her back. Terrific! She moved into the rest room proper and to one of the sinks. She turned the water on and splashed some over her face. Then she used the small paper towels to dab herself dry. Not without a momentary twinge of panic, she looked into the mirror over the sink.

Yuck! She looked terrible! Her hair was wet and stringy, her face pale and drawn. The gash down her cheek was bright red, and her other cheek looked slightly swollen from the fall to the floor.

She felt great, though. Stephanie laughed. Her vision had returned to normal, and the buzzing in her ears was gone. Okay, she ached all over, and there were cuts and bruises by the dozen, but she was alive and free again. Now she could set about making certain that Dolman paid for what he'd done.

She marched out of the women's room. Just outside it were the pay phones. Her image had taken her bag, so she didn't have money, but she didn't need any to call 911. The police could come to rescue her—and arrest Dolman.

Picking up the closest phone, she started to dial, then abruptly stopped. There was no tone. "What a time to vandalize a phone," she muttered, slamming the handset back on the hook. She lifted the second telephone and listened.

Nothing.

Surely both of them couldn't have been vandalized?

There were six phones in all, and she tried each one in turn. They were all dead. Stephanie couldn't understand it. Did the mall management turn them off at night? That didn't sound right. But it was obvious that she couldn't use any of these. Now what?

There were phones in the stores, but they were all locked up. And there were pay phones outside the mall. If she could get out the main door, she could try those. Failing that, she could always chuck a brick through a store window and set off a burglar alarm. *That* would bring the cops in a hurry!

She had started for the main doors when she became aware of a sound like the beating of wings. Sometimes birds got into the mall, but she had only heard them chirping and singing, not the rustling of their beating wings. Maybe because of the silence, the noise seemed louder?

Stephanie was in the food court now, weaving her way among tables and chairs. She glanced up, expecting to see a sparrow or something. What she did see was terrifying. A huge brass eagle was diving at her, its metallic talons outstretched, ready to dig into her flesh and claw her to shreds. The beak was open but silent, prepared to strike.

With a yell, Stephanie dived for cover under the closest table. The eagle, having missed its target, beat its great bronze wings and flew up to the ceiling again. As she stared in shock and horror, the huge bird swooped down for a fresh attack. Stephanie cowered beneath the table as the powerful talons slammed into the plastic surface, ripping and shredding it. Now the eagle began screaming, a raucous, grating sound, as it slashed the plastic into tiny shreds.

Her protection was vanishing! Stephanie rolled over, panic lending her mind speed. She grabbed one of the chairs, then jumped out from under the table, holding the chair up like a lion tamer facing one of his great cats.

The eagle spotted her movement instantly. With heavy beats of its wings, it rose again, squalling and howling. Then it dived toward her as she backed away. The talons slammed into the seat of the chair, piercing it and ripping it from her grip. The only thing that saved her face from being torn was that the eagle's claws were embedded in the chair. As it screamed and tore free, Stephanie whirled around and raced for the main entrance.

A moment later she heard the chair shatter, and the eagle was free, wings beating.

Could she make it to cover before those talons sliced into her?

The door was just twenty feet away. But it was locked, of course. Damn! Now what? She chanced a quick glance back and saw the eagle rising to muster extra force for its dive. Her eyes fastened on one of the large drumlike wastebaskets beside the glass doors. If she could lift that . . .

She threw herself to one side, terrified, as the eagle plummeted toward her. The sharp claws clicked together as they missed ripping open her skin. The eagle rose again, whirling to begin the attack once more.

And then she saw that someone else was with her in the mall.

A dark shape loomed up from among the tables and chairs. For a second she panicked, not knowing what it was. Then she gave a cry of relief.

It was the security guard, a middle-aged man. She couldn't recall his name, but he'd be on her side! "Help!" she screamed as he moved closer.

"What the hell?" he muttered, staring from her to the eagle. He must have heard the noise and come to investigate. He'd been expecting to find thieves or vandals, so he had his gun drawn. He hadn't anticipated what he did find—a lone girl hiding from a golden eagle.

The bird seemed to realize that the situation had changed. Everything created by that infernal mirror had its own dark intelligence. In midstrike the brass bird altered its angle of attack—and its target.

It plunged down toward the guard. With a muffled curse of fear, the man threw up an arm to protect his face and tried to aim at the bird with his weapon. There was the sound of a shot echoing in the empty mall, then a scream of pain and one of rage.

The bullet had missed the diving bird, but the bird had not missed the man. The brass talons ripped through the man's leather jacket, then into his flesh. Blood ran from the ruined arm, and the man fell back as the eagle struck again, fastening its claws onto his chest and tearing. As the man struggled and screamed, the great beak parted and plunged into the guard's face.

Stephanie shuddered and turned away as the bird tore at the man. The poor guard was dead in seconds. There was the sound of something metal hitting the polished floor and skidding, then the larger, wetter sound of a body being released. Sickened, Stephanie saw the unfortunate man lying in a growing pool of redness.

Between Stephanie and the body lay the man's gun.

Stephanie froze. She couldn't get out of the mall before the eagle got her, that was for certain, but she might be able to use the weapon. Did she dare try for it? She'd never even held a gun, let alone fired one—but what choice did she have? She could try to flee and die, or she could fight back.

She threw herself at the gun, fingers clawing for it as she slid across the floor. The brass bird gave a scream of outrage and then beat its huge wings. As her fingers closed around the barrel of the gun, Stephanie glanced up to see the eagle screaming down at her.

Fumbling, she managed to get her hand around the grip and her finger on the trigger. Her hand shook slightly as she raised the gun. A thought came to her mind—these things had safety catches, didn't they? She had no idea where it might be or what it looked like. Then she remembered the sound of the earlier shot—the guard must have taken the safety off! All she had to worry about was firing it.

Lying on her stomach, she used her elbows as a brace and gripped her right wrist with her left hand. That was how they always held a gun on TV shows.

She just hoped it was the right technique. Then she lined the sights up on the eagle. She had to let it get close; otherwise she'd be certain to miss. On the other hand, if the bird was *too* close and she missed, she'd be dead.

She squeezed the trigger.

Pain lanced through her wrist as the gun recoiled. Her ears rang from the sound of the shot, and she could smell the burning cordite powder. The eagle's scream was cut short in mid-dive as the bullet hit home.

In an explosion of shattering glass, the eagle fragmented. Stephanie fell behind an overturned table as sharp shards of glass showered around her and across the floor. She felt the sting of several more cuts, but at least she had survived the attack!

Which was more than that unfortunate guard had managed.

Still clutching the gun, Stephanie stumbled to her feet. Bright sparkles of glass glittered about the food court—the ruins of the eagle. The guard lay about ten feet away, but she couldn't bring herself to look at him. There was nothing she could do right now for the man. He was another victim of Dolman and that damned mirror. How many did that make now? David, Kimberly, Brent, and this man, whose name she didn't even know. How many countless others over four hundred–odd years?

Stephanie had been intent on making her escape from the mall, but she couldn't do that. Not now. Not after another death. There was something she had to do first.

She had to go back to Dolman's store and shatter that mirror. This must never happen again. And now she had a weapon and a fighting chance.

Okay, the thought of going back there scared her. But she wouldn't let her fear stop her from doing what she had to do. Forcing the fear and panic to the back of her mind, Stephanie began to retrace her steps to Dolman's.

Dolman pushed open the rear door to his store, anger and panic welling up inside him. The girl was still alive! He'd never known anyone with her cursed luck and stamina. She should have been dead three times over! Now she'd destroyed his sentinel, the eagle, his final line of defense. If she got out of the mall, she'd go straight to the police. He didn't think they'd believe her story about the mirror, but they would have to investigate two more deaths. He had to stop her before she got free. Once she was dead, he could work out what to do about the guard's body.

Crossing to the mirror, he stayed to one side of it and threw back the blanket. The mirror was the only thing that could save him now. He had to send something lethal after the girl. Looking around the room, he desperately sought inspiration. The suits of armor in the shop would have been perfect, but they were too heavy to bring in. He would have to use something smaller.

His eyes lit on an ornate candlestick, with a tripod base—three legs. He grabbed it and hastily lit the candle. Placing it on the table in front of the mirror, he watched the duplicate candlestick form. The metal legs of the image shivered and then flexed. Leaping down from the table, the candlestick trotted out of the store, seeking its target.

Bringing the metal object to life had taken another slice of his life. Dolman could feel the wrinkles form in his face as his thick hair grew thin and start graying. It was a heavy price to pay, but if he didn't stop Stephanie from fleeing, he'd be dead anyway. Feverishly, he searched for something else to animate and send after her in case the candlestick failed.

The parking lot was dark and empty when Nicki pulled Scott's car to a halt by the main doors. The sodium-vapor lights cast a glow across the expanse of asphalt, but there were only a couple of cars—probably abandoned—in the huge lot. Lights were on inside the mall, as always, but there was no sign of life.

The journey over had been long enough for Scott to have recovered. As soon as the car stopped, he was out and running. Nicki followed, not even bothering to remove the keys from the ignition. Both of them came to a halt beside the great glass doors. Scott jerked on them futilely. They were locked.

"Damn!" he muttered. "We've got to get in there, Nicki! Steph's in danger. I know she is."

"There must be a security guard on duty," Nicki

replied, peering through the glass. She started to hammer on the door. "Maybe he'll hear us."

Scott waited impatiently for a moment, hammering his fists on another of the glass panes. "I can't wait any longer," he announced. "We've got to get inside!"

"How?" asked Nicki. "It's locked."

There was an ornamental flower bed close to the entrance, with a large Welcome sign embedded between the flowers and the rocks. Scott strode over to it and picked up a rock the size of a dinner plate. Despite the weight, he hefted it, then walked back closer to the entrance. Nicki jumped as he threw the rock at the glass door.

The rock crashed through the door, scattering huge shards of glass all over. Instantly an alarm bell started to sound. Ignoring this, Scott kicked out the fragments of shattered glass. "It's not locked now," he told her.

Feeling a guilty thrill as well as a knot of fear, Nicki bent low and climbed through the broken door after him. The alarm was bound to bring the police. She only hoped that she and Scott could find Stephanie and rescue her before they had to explain what they were up to.

Scott suddenly stopped dead and pointed. Nicki bumped into him before she could stop. Following his gesture, she saw a figure lying in a pool of drying blood, shards of glass scattered across the floor beside the body. For a second she was terrified that they were too late to save Stephanie, but then she saw that it was the slashed body of the security guard.

"Poor guy," muttered Scott.

Nicki nodded. She was starting to get used to the sight of dead bodies, and that really spooked her. She felt sad for the man, but she was glad it wasn't her friend. "Dolman's is right down this hall ahead," she told Scott.

"Come on," he said, running.

As she sprinted along after him, she heard the crack of a gunshot ahead.

Stephanie was getting the hang of the gun. This time her wrist didn't hurt. The wreckage of the animated candlestick now lay glittering on the floor ahead. How many more of these traps did Dolman have waiting for her?

She pressed on, warily watching for any more signs of movement. She'd heard a crash from the direction of the main doors a moment or two earlier, but she couldn't afford to go back to investigate. Then the alarm had sounded. That meant the police were on their way. She *had* to destroy the mirror before they arrived! If one of the cops unwittingly glanced into the mirror, who knew what the result would be?

Carefully she drew closer to the antique store. As she did so, another object darted out of the shop. This was one of those ugly Chinese porcelain dogs. Growling and yapping, teeth bared, the monstrosity hurled itself at her.

She leveled the gun and fired.

The mirror-dog exploded. Barely pausing, she

205

stepped over the glass fragments and approached the shop door.

A mannequin threw itself through the gap, its face impassive, its hands extended to grab her.

Stephanie jumped, then raised the gun and pulled the trigger.

Nothing. She was out of bullets!

Before she could dodge the attack, the dummy fastened its hands around her throat. She gave a strangled cry as the mannequin shoved her to the floor and started to throttle her. Stephanie struggled, trying to strike out at the plastic creature. But the pressure on her throat wouldn't let up, and she could feel the cold fingers bearing down on her windpipe, choking her. Great yellow spots began dancing across her vision, and she knew she couldn't survive this time.

Then another shape hurled itself into sight. She could vaguely make out a long leg as it whipped out, kicking the dummy hard in the head. The hands tore free from her neck as the mannequin went flying. Blinking, Stephanie gulped in deep breaths, trying to recover. Arms slipped about her, and then she could make out Nicki helping her up. Beyond Nicki, Scott had picked up a wastebasket and slammed it down heavily on the fallen dummy's head.

There was the now familiar sound of breaking glass, and the mannequin exploded under the impact.

Rubbing her throat to try to relieve some of the pain, Stephanie looked at her two friends with gratitude and relief. "Thanks, guys," she croaked. "Talk about timing."

"Talk about messes," muttered Nicki, grinning. "This is certainly one fine mess."

"You okay?" Scott asked her anxiously.

Stephanie shook her head. "No, not really. But I'll survive. Later on, you can tell me how you got here. Right now I've got to destroy a mirror." She started to move forward, but Scott blocked her way.

"You've done enough," he told her. "I'll take over. What are we going after?"

"Dolman's got a mirror that duplicates things and brings them to life," she told him urgently. "It's in the back room of his store. Whatever you do, don't look into it! And you've got to be careful. He's trying real hard to kill us with anything he can."

"I'll be careful," Scott promised. He slid inside the shop.

Stephanie gave Nicki's hand a squeeze and followed. Nicki, eyes flickering around nervously, trailed along. The gloom inside hadn't improved, but Stephanie could hear sounds from the back room. Dolman had come here and was setting anything he could after her!

As Scott moved past the counter, there was a blur of motion. He jumped aside, but he wasn't quite fast enough. A small creature—some kind of Oriental dragon statue—hissed and snapped at him as it leaped from the darkness. The fangs of the creature missed their first target—Scott's throat—but sank into his shoulder instead. With a yell of agony, Scott fell to the floor, trying to shove the creature away. The dragon's tail snaked about his arm and jerked.

With a scream of fury, Stephanie leaped to help. The empty gun was still in her hand, and she smashed it down on the writhing dragon-thing. The little monster shattered into glass fragments, and Scott was free.

His shoulder was a mess, however. Blood was bubbling out of the gash the dragon had chewed, and Scott was pale and shaken. Stephanie ripped at his T-shirt, tearing it away. Wadding the cloth up, she pressed it into the wound and put his hand over it.

"Stay here," she ordered, more intent than ever on settling things with Dolman. As Scott started to protest, she shook her head. "Don't argue," she ordered.

With Nicki at her side, she entered the back room. Dolman was there, trying to drag one of the suits of armor into line with the mirror. He wasn't having much luck, which was fortunate. The thought of facing a knight in full combat gear terrified Stephanie. Hearing the girls enter, Dolman looked up, panting.

Stephanie gasped. He'd changed again—aging this time. He was barely more than a skeleton covered in thin, dry skin. His pale blue eyes burned, bulging from their skeletal sockets. His hair was barely wisps of snow on his head. His fingers were bone-thin, and his veins stood out blue against the alabaster skin. He looked almost every day of his four hundred and fifty years.

"You won't beat me," he gasped. "I won't let you escape."

"I'm not escaping," Stephanie said coldly. "I'm here to finish this."

"No," he cawed, his voice thin and harsh. "I won't let you! I won't!"

"It's too late," Stephanie told him. With a growl, she pushed hard on the armor. Losing his balance, Dolman crashed to the floor, the armor pinning him down. He gave a thin cry of pain, struggling to get free.

Ignoring the weak, disgusting old man, Stephanie wrenched the sword out of the armor's hands. Then, taking a deep breath, she stepped forward and swung the blade with all of her energy against the great mirror.

In the second before impact, the carved shapes in the mirror's frame seemed to quiver and shake with life, as if the mirror were struggling to move itself out of the path of the blow. There was a terrible, unearthly keening—the baying of all the hounds of hell—and then Stephanie's arm was jolted as the blade crashed into the mirror.

Into a billion fragments, the mirror exploded, spewing glass shards everywhere. She fell flat to the floor, dragging Nicki down beside her, and received only a few more nicks, but both girls were beyond complaining. The sword clattered to the floor amid the shower of glass.

At the same second Dolman gave a soul-rattling, inhuman scream—and exploded also. The armor collapsed, tinkling, atop the mound of glass that had been Dolman.

Nicki raised her eyes to stare in horror at the shambles. *"He* was one of those reflections," she gasped.

Wearily, Stephanie managed to turn around. "It makes sense," she said. "He told me he'd found the mirror hundreds of years ago. He would have looked into it, naturally—and produced his own evil reflection. The real Dolman must have died then. The reflection lived on in his place."

"But with the mirror gone, its power has been shattered also," Nicki finished. "He fell apart. . . ." She gave a shudder.

"Speaking of falling apart," Stephanie admitted, "I think I may just do that. I feel lousy."

"You look it, too," said Nicki, a faint smile tugging at her lips. Nothing kept her down for long! "Maybe I should make a move on your guy. For once, I look better than you."

"Don't you dare."

Nicki laughed. "Not me. I've seen your evil side, remember? I know what you're capable of doing. There's no way I'm ever going to annoy you!"

Stephanie shook her head as she staggered back to join Scott. "I'll never be able to live down what that image did."

"Don't try," Nicki suggested. "I think both Henry Blake and Shelly have learned valuable lessons from her."

"Me, too," agreed Scott. He was pale, but he'd managed to hang on to his wits. "I had a chance to see you the way I thought I wanted you. And I discovered that I prefer you just the way you are."

Stephanie collapsed next to him. She managed to lean over and kiss his nose. "And I like you the way you are."

Nicki wrinkled her nose in mock disgust. "Yech! If you two are going to get all mushy, I'm going to look for the cops." She sighed. "It won't be easy to explain what happened."

"You do it, Nicki," Scott suggested. "You've got friends in high places."

"Mom and Dad?" she asked incredulously. "I'll get jailed for life." Then she shook her head ruefully. "Okay, I'll see what I can do. Maybe I can talk them into letting us share a cell or something."

"The tape recorder," Stephanie remembered. "Dolman put it on his counter. I taped his confession earlier. I don't think he erased it."

Nicki grinned. "Well, that should help. Hang in there." She left the store. Stephanie heard her footsteps recede down the hall.

Scott managed to look at Stephanie. "How do you feel?" he gasped.

"Honestly?" She shook her head. "Terrible. But it'll pass. Some things won't." She gripped his hand in hers. "Luckily."

# About the Author

JOHN PEEL was born in Nottingham, England, the oldest of seven children, and he attended Nottingham University. He moved to the United States to marry his pen pal, Nan. They live in Manorville, New York, with their wire-haired fox terrier, Dashiell, who frequently wants John to stop writing to play ball. John is the author of numerous science fiction and mystery novels for young adults, and he has been a contributing editor and writer for several magazines. His novels *Talons* and *Shattered* are available from Archway Paperbacks. He is currently working on his next novel, *Poison*.